Flames and Thorns

The Orion Dynasty Book 1

CK Franco

Blurbs

He's the enemy I should hate.

But his touch feels like fire I can't escape.

Caius Drake built his empire on ruthless ambition and control. To the world, he's untouchable. To me, Seraphina Hayes, he's the man who betrayed me—the only one who ever burned me deep enough to leave scars.

Now, fate forces us back into each other's orbit. Every look is a battle, every touch a war, every kiss a dangerous spark.

But in the shadows of the Orion Brotherhood, secrets cut sharper than knives, and love is the deadliest weakness of all.

Enemies. Lovers. Betrayal and desire.
We were never meant to survive each other...
And yet, the fire between us refuses to die.

To every dreamer who dared to rise above fear,
to every soul who carried hope even in the darkest of nights,
and to every fighter who refused to surrender—
this book is for you.
May these words remind you that no mountain is too high,
no storm is too fierce,
and no dream is ever too impossible
when your heart burns with purpose.
Keep going. The world needs your light.

"Some bonds are forged in fire, others in blood—but the rarest are sealed by the heart."

Prologue

Power is not inherited—it is taken. In the brotherhood's world of glass towers and unbreakable vows, secrets burn hotter than desire. He was fire, she was the thorn that drew his blood—and together they would ignite a love too dangerous to be contained.

Contents

Collision of Worlds

Seraphina Hayes quietly enters a large, cold building that feels more like a fortress than an office. The lobby stretches out before her, colder than the morning outside. She instinctively touches the strap of her worn messenger bag, a small sign that she comes from a different world. The marble floor is so shiny that it blurs her reflection. Above, circular LED lights hang, casting a white glow that brightens every corner without being too harsh.

Along one wall, black leather seats sit neatly, unused. Metal sculptures with strange shapes stand in shadowy corners, their shiny surfaces reflecting ghostly images onto the floor. Staff members move carefully in black suits, appearing like clockwork, full of purpose. Their footsteps speak a language Seraphina hasn't learned yet.

She stands still, feeling the weight of many silent expectations, like the thick glass surrounding the building. This place is for people who fit in—who believe in control and power, who act without doubt. Her heart beats quietly, not from fear, but from excitement mixed with stubbornness.

The sharp sound of heels breaks the quiet. Ms. Patel appears, every detail of her outfit perfect according to the Drake Empire's strict rules. "Welcome, Ms. Hayes," she says, her voice calm but efficient.

Seraphina answers, feeling heat rise in her face as she meets Ms. Patel's steady gaze. The woman gives her a security badge, cold in Seraphina's palm. Together, they walk to a glass security gate. A scanner lights up, and the badge opens the door. Inside, long hallways smell of toner and cold air. Every worker looks tough—wearing dark suits and serious faces. There is no color here, only clear purpose.

Questions run through Seraphina's mind. What will she lose here? What part of her holds tight to her past, to softness and color, to feeling different? She remembers being a teenager, the only one with paint on her jeans at a friend's clean house, or riding a bus to art shows she couldn't afford. But this place is different. What happens here is not just about dreams or talent, but about surviving a silent, complicated game.

At the work area, Ms. Patel quickly introduces her to Olivia Barnes. Olivia's handshake is firm, matching her sharp suit. "We'll be working together," she says, her eyes quickly judging Seraphina—warm but cold at once. Behind Olivia, Zach Matthews leans closer, whispering, "Mistakes are not repeated here." Though he smiles slightly, his warning remains clear.

Seraphina's heart races, but she stands a little taller.

They take the elevator up. It's quiet and glassy, each floor passing slowly. The city below grows smaller.

Ms. Patel opens the last door. Caius Drake stands by the big window, wearing a black suit, lit by bright white light that makes him seem like a legend rather than a man. The office is simple—chrome and wood, neat and empty. He turns, his eyes gray and cold. The room feels smaller.

"Ms. Hayes. Welcome to Drake Investment Empire." His voice is controlled and firm.

Seraphina puts her portfolio on the glass desk, her heart pounding. He looks through her work carefully. "You use bold colors and unusual designs."

She lifts her chin, a challenge in her voice. "Good brands don't copy others."

"In our world, risk isn't rewarded," Caius says flatly. "We sell trust, not new ideas."

Seraphina meets his eyes. "Sometimes trust grows from standing out. Clients remember what breaks the pattern."

He pauses, then pushes the portfolio aside like a fragile object. "We value efficiency and predictability. To succeed here, you must change quickly."

The air feels cold, like biting her tongue during a fight. Caius ends the meeting firmly. "Your first project starts this afternoon. Ms. Patel will tell you."

The door closes behind her. The badge presses into her hand, leaving small marks. Seraphina walks back, her jaw tight with quiet determination. Each step shakes off doubt. Glass and steel weigh on her shoulders. She doesn't look back.

The boardroom shows everything the city wants to be: shiny glass, cold details, and the feeling of honesty. Light breaks across the long table, splitting Seraphina's reflection into many pieces as she enters. Her footsteps echo on the marble floor, matching her fast heart. Executives turn as one, sharp eyes on her. Caius Drake looks at her with cold gray eyes, hands folded as if he controls the air. To his right, Olivia sits straight, green eyes calmly studying her. To his left, Marcus Langston remains calm, quiet but watchful.

Numbers fill the screen as Caius starts the meeting. His voice is clear and strong: "Brand growth is about careful changes. Our clients want steady, proven results." Slides show past campaigns—blue finance logos, rising graphs, simple slogans. The room cools with each number, colors fading to gray.

Seraphina rests her hands on her closed sketchbook. She breathes in the smell of glass and machines, aftershave and stress. She thinks of late nights at broken desks, pitching bright ideas to doubtful nonprofits, leading product launches that shook old stories. She remembers how a bold stroke could break expectations and build trust. Her thumb traces the cover, grounding her.

Caius moves to the last chart, lips tight. "Questions now."

Seraphina raises her hand, breaking the room's quiet. Pens stop tapping, suits still—air holds. She knows all eyes are on her, wary and guessing, but she speaks clearly. "I suggest we try a bolder plan. Strong fonts, moving designs that change with the user. Recent data shows this gets more attention." She points to the screen. "It's measurable, though different."

For a moment, no one speaks. Olivia's lips tighten. Zach looks toward the exit. Someone shifts nervously.

Caius breaks the silence. "Our clients aren't art fans, Ms. Hayes. Your idea is risky. It's naive for this sector. Corporate brands need stability, not show."

His tone is smooth, almost polite.

Seraphina sees the careful looks, the unspoken calculations—no one surprises Caius, and those who try often lose. She holds his gaze.

"I'm not talking about show," she says. "Brands live in the real world. I've helped groups reach new people with honest, original images, not just safe math. Triad Greenway went from ignored to known by being bold."

Some executives glance at each other, curious but cautious. Olivia leans forward, pen paused. Marcus's face shows little, but respect hints at his jaw.

Caius interrupts. "We are not Triad Greenway. At Drake, results come before creative risks. The market punishes change." He remains still, firm. "Our methods show stability. Our name demands it. I won't risk client trust now."

A heavy quiet fills the room. Seraphina straightens, her sketchbook firm in her hands. Experience teaches her she has heard *no* before—told to stay inside invisible lines. Her wrist's tattoo, a thorned rose, reminds her of strength earned in struggle. She won't back down.

Marcus speaks gently but firmly. "Creativity can improve strategy, Caius. Let's pause this and move to client assets. Different views bring wisdom." His words ease the tension, guiding the group forward.

In the pause, teams begin to form—some follow Marcus's calm, others stick with Caius's strictness—the future conflicts taking shape. Seraphina feels the shifting ground beneath the polished floor.

The meeting continues, but the tension remains. Every look and word carries meaning. Caius speaks briefly, Olivia writes quickly, and Marcus nods as he keeps the flow. The team matches this energy, careful yet energized.

When the meeting ends, Seraphina stands with her sketchbook ready. She steps out into the hall, sharp air and narrowed eyes. The excitement of the fight burns on her skin. She refuses to be small.

Behind her, Caius talks quietly to Olivia, already planning the next steps. The quiet swallows up the last sounds of the boardroom fight, but the memory stays—a sign that the struggle at Drake Investment Empire has only begun.

Late morning light fills the open workspace, a glass room high above the city noise. Workers gather around tall desks, wearing dark suits that move like a dance. The LED lights shine softly on metal and glass, tinting briefcases, hair, and hands with a cold glow.

Caius Drake appears, a steady presence against the city view. He calls for attention with a hand and speaks clearly, like a clock ticking. "For new accounts, we must work with our Orion Club contacts. Some decisions wait for their approval. Expect delays—unless you want to cause more." Hearing this, people pause—eyes flick quickly, nervous, before returning to work. Laptops click. Phones light up. The moment fades but leaves behind a feeling of worry.

Seraphina stands at the edge, her badge warm in her hand. A chill slides down her wrist. There is a hidden power here—like underground rivers that guide everything seen. She watches two project managers slip away. One looks back sharply before disappearing. Their voices come faintly as she passes.

"The Orion names don't get shared, not unless you're in."

"She's new. Maybe she'll learn the smart way."

"Or vanish. Loyalty is everything—Caius makes sure." The half-joke isn't funny. They look at Seraphina long enough for her heart to skip. She moves on, the voices fading into typing and printer hums.

Seraphina knows these stories are like secret rules—power passed in whispers and silence. The Orion Club isn't just rumor. It's control and order; it's the wall that tests every dream and act of freedom. She feels its weight after Caius's words—pressing on each choice and conversation. The club connects not only to Drake Investment but also to the city, where money and loyalty mix, their lines blurred.

At the coffee station, steam rises from a black cup. The smell of strong, almost burnt coffee fills the air. Zach Matthews shows up, his suit too new, his smile tight. He waits until her cup shakes slightly, then leans in.

"Don't drop your guard," he whispers. "Here, the worst thing isn't missing a deadline. It's being unpredictable." His eyes lock with hers, soft but warning. "The last creative hire didn't even last three paychecks. No word. Just gone." His smile almost breaks.

"Trying to scare me?" Seraphina's voice is sharper than she intends.

"No. Just warning." Zach looks around before lowering his voice. "People disappear. But their stories stay. Keep low. Play the game. At least until you know who not to cross."

She holds his gaze, unmoved. "Thanks, but playing along isn't my style."

"I hope you're tougher than you seem," he says, worry clear on his face.

He leaves her with more questions than answers.

At noon, she slips out past security and through glass doors, feeling many eyes on her. The sun heats the sidewalk, traffic buzzing. Seraphina sits on the steps, the busy world rushing by. She sips bitter coffee and lets quiet fill her.

In these towers, people like Caius control more than money—they make deals, redraw power lines of privilege and exclusion. The Orion Club is not just a place but a network of invisible hands. It shapes the city, decides elections, hides enemies, protects friends, and pushes out those who won't obey. Here, deals made in dark lounges can exile more than a job. The rules are in every look and silence. For a newcomer, the code is both warning and invitation—a constant challenge to understand or be pushed aside.

Seraphina holds her coffee cup, her thumb circling the rim. She wonders what it costs to belong and what she must give up. The city's noise won't drown out old fears—the wish to fit in fighting the need to stay herself. Yet beneath her caution is a strong, uneasy excitement. Something inside wants to see behind the curtain, to know why even the strongest bow to the club's power. She looks at her reflection in the glass, seeing many versions of herself—one woman standing just outside the game.

The coffee is gone, leaving a sour taste. Sunlight catches the building's edge in gold. Seraphina stands, a breeze lifting her hair, and walks back inside—wariness curling inside her, but curiosity pulling her forward into the tower's center.

Walls and Defiance

Light shines on the black table as Seraphina sits at the far end, her sketchbook closed on top of her tablet. The conference room feels cold and quiet, the air filtered, and the silence is almost like that of a hospital room, broken only by the soft humming of the air conditioning. The shiny metal edges of the room reflect the city outside, which seems full of unseen energy—a reminder of the world they all serve or fear. Caius stands at the head of the table, his suit perfectly pressed and his movements controlled. Abstract sculptures sit in the corners, showcasing order and control. The faint smell of bergamot tea mixes with the scent of the city below.

A screen at the end of the table changes slides, casting a blue light on the faces in the room. Caius's eyes are cold as he speaks, giving sharp and clear orders about "brand alignment," "market uniformity," and "compliance." These terms mean making the brand look the same everywhere while following the rules carefully. He requests changing the logo to be simpler, dulling the colors, and removing the hand-drawn style that makes it unique. Changing it this way would take the life out of it, rendering it dull and gray.

Seraphina feels her heart beat fast. She bites her tongue, an old habit when she's trying to stay strong. Around her, people quietly shuffle their papers and tap their pens; one man keeps bouncing his knee nervously. No one looks at her—they've learned it's safer not to.

She places her hands flat on the cold table to steady herself. When she speaks, her voice is plain. "With respect, these changes erase the meaning. The design is supposed to feel alive, not just fit a set pattern. If we remove its feeling, it becomes empty and lifeless." Her fingers twitch, but she remains still. She meets Caius's eyes, seeing her own reflection in the glass beside her.

A nervous feeling spreads through the room. One assistant leans over his notes so closely that his glasses almost fall. A woman looks away, pretending to focus on her computer screen. The air feels sharp and metallic, and the city's distant noise is quiet and lonely.

Caius leans back slowly, his chair barely making a sound. He looks serious, his steel-gray eyes narrowing. His finger taps once on the shiny armrest before stopping. A scar above his eyebrow catches the light.

"You don't understand what matters here," he says quietly, his voice sharp. "Every project is more than just art. Our clients want everything to match and be consistent. I advise you, Ms. Hayes, not to mix personal creativity with the rules of a company worth billions. If you want to succeed, rethink your approach."

Seraphina straightens up, her hands wide on the table, determination growing inside her. She has faced this before—in rooms full of judgment, told to tone down her style. But this time feels more serious. Falling into the background is a danger she won't accept. Giving in means losing not just this project but the chance to prove her work can thrive in this strict world.

She stares at Caius. "Why is control always the goal? If real impact matters, why remove anything surprising? How can you build a world people believe in if you only want everything to look the same?"

For a moment, the room is completely still, the air heavy like before a storm. The team, pretending to take notes, freezes, afraid to show interest or take sides. Papers rustle as one man fidgets, and a woman holds her breath. Open resistance is not allowed—it breaks the smooth surface Caius tries to maintain.

But Seraphina keeps looking at him, her question hanging between them like pollen. She knows the risk—her position is shaky, the ground uncertain. Still, she would rather leave with nothing than lose the style that makes her work hers.

She grabs her sketchbook, collecting her stylus and tablet in one smooth move. "If real connection isn't wanted here," she says quietly, "maybe I'm in the wrong place." Her chair scrapes loudly on the floor. She stands, straight-backed, and walks past the silent faces—some scared, some watching with secret admiration.

She reaches the door without stopping, letting fresh air in as she leaves. At the table, Caius gestures sharply, and the meeting breaks into quiet talk, the tension still hanging in the air.

Caius walks down the hallway, his shoes soft on the marble floor. The quiet around him makes his frustration grow louder. Cameras flash red lights, and glass doors shine. He passes spotless white benches and sharp metal decorations that feel like warnings. At the end, his office door opens quietly; the city spreads out beneath dusk-lit windows. He pulls off his tie sharply and lets it drop on the polished wood desk. His jaw tightens, fingers pressing into his pants, eyes drawn to the neat abstract sculptures that don't judge him.

Caius thinks about Seraphina in the meeting—her steady voice, hands flat on the glass table, eyes unblinking under pressure. He expected some resistance, but not such strong defiance. Most people give in eventually. But she fights back like a wild wave—unpredictable. For a moment, he feels out of control, a chill running through him.

A quiet knock at the door. Marcus steps in, looking calm and serious, his suit neat against the low light. He stops at the desk, carrying nothing to break the tension.

Caius speaks first, his voice low and tight. "She refused every important change. She told everyone that my edits would ruin her work." He turns to look at the city, the sun touching tall buildings with soft orange light.

Marcus waits, reading the feelings behind Caius's cold words. He takes a slow breath. "Did you expect her to follow orders without question?"

"Not that easy. But not this open defiance," Caius replies. His voice shows frustration and a hidden respect for her, quickly controlled.

Marcus's face shows nothing, but his calm presence feels like an anchor. "If you wanted someone who just obeys, you would have hired someone else. You knew she would stand for her work. Maybe you wanted that."

Caius doesn't admit the truth in Marcus's words. He lets silence fill the room, thick with memories and the city's far-off noise. Still, he can't shake his respect for Seraphina's refusal to be shaped. She turns problems into purpose. This breaks the order Caius has built carefully over time.

"Let me be clear, Caius. Forcing her to make dull changes will kill what you prized when you hired her. She might stay, but the project—and her spirit—will die. You don't want another dead campaign with no life," Marcus says calmly but firmly.

Caius's hands clench behind his back. The need to take control again is strong and familiar—a wall between him and the risks that once nearly destroyed him. But there is rebellion in the choice: what if giving up some control brings not chaos, but greatness? It's risky to think that, but Seraphina's fight has lit a fire in the dull routine. Her strength is wild, but it could make the company more than just strong—unforgettable.

He breathes out slowly. "You think I should let her do whatever she wants? Trust unpredictability to help the project?"

"I think you set the basic rules—and let her work right up to the edge. Your reputation is built on control. Maybe now it's time to try influence. She isn't a threat unless you make her one."

Quiet fills the room, blending with the coming night, swallowing old beliefs. Caius walks to the window. Glass and steel glow in gold and purple light over the city's heart. Below, his world moves forward on tracks of profit and order. But in his reflection, another truth shines: even the strongest empire can break if its leader is too rigid.

He thinks about Seraphina's challenge, feeling a small respect for it. In her true self, there is power—a different kind than cold control. Could a leader allow this wildness without losing control? Could he change his leadership to guide while letting new ideas grow?

This path is new and risky. But if it works—if he lets her light join his ambition—maybe his legacy will be more than numbers and past wins. Maybe he can build something untouchable.

He turns from the window, doubt stiff in his spine.

"What if she confuses freedom with weakness? What if others see my choice as splitting?"

"There's a difference between giving in to chaos and guiding it. You're not losing power—just changing how you use it. The right people will understand. The rest aren't worth worrying about."

Caius's jaw relaxes a little. "We set the basics for the campaign. She fills in the rest. She gets freedom. We keep the structure."

Marcus nods. "You'll get more from her that way. And maybe from yourself."

Marcus leaves, the door closing softly. Alone, Caius stays by the window, the city lights glowing as night grows. He stands, thinking about a new kind of leadership—where control is a direction, not a shield. Below, lights turn on one by one, the world getting ready for night and change.

Under the Glass Tower

The elevator doors opened quietly, and Seraphina stepped into the shiny marble lobby of the Drake Investment Empire. The cold floor touched her shoes as she paused, inhaling the clean, expensive air. She tucked a loose strand of hair behind her ear, trying not to show her nervousness. The ceiling was very high, with soft gray light emanating from hidden panels. Black leather benches lined the room like pieces on a chessboard. The security desk was plain but glowed with blue light, standing firm between her and the rest of the building.

An assistant in a dark suit approached, holding a silver tablet. "Ms. Hayes?" Her voice was calm and professional. Seraphina nodded, searching for any sign of warmth on the woman's perfect face.

"I'm Lila. Welcome to Drake Investment Empire. We'll start your tour soon," Lila said with a careful smile. "Mr. Drake wants you to see every department related to your design contract. If you need a break, just let me know." She glanced at a hidden earpiece, her lips moving slightly. Seraphina felt the quiet watchfulness behind her words.

Lila led her down a glass hallway that divided the lobby into public and private areas. Their footsteps echoed softly on the stone. Black leather seats along the walls resembled art—firm and sharp. The glass walls displayed the city outside, while tiny cameras in the corners watched quietly.

Her heart raced. This place was a world away from the cozy café with its worn floors, clinking spoons, and rough laughter. Here, voices were low and urgent, and everyone moved quickly and carefully. Art pieces made of twisted metal reflected the energy of ambition. Everything was spotless and precise, with a purpose just beneath the surface.

They stopped by a huge window showing the city spread out like a board game. The sun shone on glass buildings and a river far below. Tiny cars moved like ants. There was no smell of coffee or pastries here, just the sharp scent of electricity.

"Mr. Drake likes things clear and open," Lila said. "Transparency is key. You can see all the bosses' offices, but you can't enter without permission." Her words were brief, hinting at strict rules.

Ahead, through a glass wall, Seraphina saw busy teams gathered around glowing tables, screens filled with charts, speaking in fast languages she barely understood. They wore dark suits and sharp shoes, their faces focused. No paint or sketchbooks were in sight—just laptops and control. Everything moved like a perfectly timed dance.

Workers passed by with serious expressions, holding tablets close like shields. They spoke quietly, always connected to devices in their ears. There was a silent code in how they moved—a rule of power and control that Seraphina couldn't fully grasp.

Power filled the air here quietly but strongly. No mess, no wild creativity—only the feeling of being watched—by cameras, rivals, and the glass itself. Her breath fogged the window, the only soft thing in this hard place.

A conference room with clear walls revealed a meeting in progress. They seemed to speak with sharp words like weapons. Seraphina didn't recognize anyone and doubted they'd know her.

Lila pointed to a line of private offices. "Drake likes order," she said. "Everything follows his style—methodical, firm, and strict." Voices echoed behind the doors as if choreographed. Even silence felt heavy, full of expectation.

They stopped before a tall glass door with steel edges. Frosted glass showed only a faint outline of a desk inside. "This is Mr. Drake's office," Lila said quietly, as if the walls might hear. "He works from here—watching and judging. This room is the center of everything. What he says can change lives."

Seraphina stayed by the door, looking at her reflection—small, brave, unsure. The air felt thick. She imagined Caius Drake behind the door, his gray eyes seeing everything, judging the world by standards she couldn't name. Her shoulders tightened. The warm, messy world of the café felt very far away.

She took a deep breath, touched the steel edge, then followed Lila's steady steps, feeling the cold promise of the glass building behind her.

The quiet by the big window was softer than the rest of the building—like the air was waiting for something. Seraphina wrapped herself in this calm. The city stretched below, a mix of bright lights, tall towers, and sunlight on rooftops. She pressed her hand against the cool glass, feeling the hum of elevators and machines throughout the building.

The smell was not coffee but something sharp—like electricity in the air. The glass was so clear that her reflection flickered like a ghost. She saw herself softened by light, but her navy blouse and neat pants felt stiff—like a costume, not her usual clothes. She studied herself: hair pinned back, a tattoo half-hidden by a watch she wouldn't normally wear, lips pressed tight. At home, she would move freely with sleeves stained by charcoal dust. Now, she felt like she was living someone else's role.

She thought of the café: sunlight streaming through old brick windows, dust floating above worn tables, the sound of people laughing, the steam from coffee, and the smell of cinnamon scones. The warm air there lingered on her clothes like a shield. She remembered the feel of paper under her hand as she sketched—a quick line, a curl of a rose or a wing—and the way her heart lifted when colors filled the blank page. Here, in the silent towers, those bright mornings felt like a story from another life.

The loud click of heels on the marble floor reminded her that she didn't belong here. Everything felt planned, every step careful—as if mistakes or weak feelings had no place. She felt the heavy pressure of expectations. The city outside glowed with opportunity, but the chance felt like a storm, not a sunrise.

Her reflection caught her full attention—a stranger wearing fine clothes. Doubt tightened inside her. She remembered Jasper teasing her about "grown-up dress-up" when she practiced walking in heels, wobbling on the hardwood floor. She had laughed, hugged him tight, and said her stubbornness was a superpower. But deep down, she feared the city would swallow what made her special—that she would become just another sharp, quiet face fading into the glass walls.

She let out a soft breath and closed her eyes. Her heartbeat matched the city's—steady and fast. Why had she said yes? She remembered Lillian's kind words, her mother's strong hand holding hers late at night. She smelled steam and cinnamon again, sitting at the worn café table, bringing light to paint in the gray of winter. She remembered why: she wanted more. To put her colors on something bigger than napkin sketches, to prove that art and her true self could exist anywhere if she tried hard enough.

She breathed in deeply, making space in the tight feeling.

"Scared?" she whispered. "Or just waking up?"

She stood taller, imagining Jasper's teasing but loving words—words that said she was more than any cage. She smoothed her blouse until it felt right. Her fingers touched the rose tattoo on her wrist, tracing the thorn for courage.

"It'll be fine, Sera. You've faced harder things," she said quietly, believing it.

The memory of the café—music, laughter, small magic in everyday life—flowed under the hard surface of her new world. She imagined bringing her bold style to corporate presentations: bright colors, open spaces, a bit of rebellion in the dull gray. Let them stare. She would not become plain. Art was the tough plant growing through concrete. She owed it to that girl in the café.

She squared her shoulders, steady among the marble and steel. She picked up her bag, holding it like a promise. Her eyes met the endless city, and she imagined a place where she belonged—not despite her colors, but because of them.

She stepped away from the window with quiet determination, already planning how she would enter the new world down the hallway.

Seraphina moved along a quiet hallway. The cold glass and steel softened as she turned into a small lounge. The air felt warmer here, full of green plants twisting around chrome stands and reaching toward small windows shaded by clouds. Metal sculptures twisted among the plants, catching light from hidden lamps. The distant noise of the city was faint, replaced by the quiet life growing under the soil in the pots.

She sank into a soft moss-green sofa, feeling some tension leave her shoulders. She pulled her bag onto her lap, its worn strap and ink stains out of place in this neat room. Her fingers opened a zipper and pulled out her old sketchbook—scuffed and taped together with pages thick from use and old damage. The pages were soft in her hands like a callus.

She flipped through old drawings—colorful city scenes, strange creatures with wings, a blue mandala drawn after a sleepless night. These pages were proof of her survival—old marks crossed out and new ideas written over them. She stopped at one drawing she couldn't ignore: a single rose, dark and heavy, wrapped in sharp thorns. The ink smudged down the stem as if the flower had bled.

Her finger traced the outline—the red petals on a black stem, the thorns curling tightly. Memories came flooding back: the kitchen light at 2 a.m., her pencil scratching over paper, her body worn out with worry. That night, the commission she hoped for—her chance to stop working three café shifts a day—was lost in a cold email. Her dream of being a full-time artist vanished with one message. Rent was late, and the burnt taste of espresso lingered. Hope felt fragile, like dying rose petals on a windowsill.

Had she known then that nights like this would return? That longing would become both a friend and an enemy, pulling her into places like this one—clean, fancy spaces where creativity was business, not magic? The rose was her yes to fighting back. Each thorn showed how she held on to who she was, refusing to let her art be watered down to fit in, even as bills weighed her down.

She could almost smell that night—the kitchen smells, the cold ink, the city rain outside her old window. Her chest tightened with the memory—a pain and comfort at once. She had made it through with sheer will, driven by the belief that raw beauty could be her answer to loss. But even now, in this fake oasis, doubt beat inside her—wondering if joining this world meant losing something important.

Around her, the plants seemed to reach toward her. She thought of her mother's kitchen, herb plants spilling over windowsills, sunlight dusted with flour. The café world was full of friendly chaos—lipstick marks on cups, poems written on napkins. That world was paused now, traded for this place of order and ambition. Her clothes shaped her differently; her body's lines made a statement, not comfort. Every button hid her.

She turned the page. Notes in the margin caught her eye: "don't give up," "keep your edge"—words she wrote on nights she faltered. Her hands remembered counting money, trading for paint, choosing between food and art supplies. She grew stronger in that struggle: instead of giving up her style to fit in, she fought to keep her uniqueness, knowing the other choice was silence.

If she gave in, let her edges fade, she'd disappear in these mirrored towers. But if she held on—kept the pain of rejection and the rush of risk—maybe she could find a new place inside Caius Drake's fortress. She wanted to change things, not vanish.

Seraphina breathed deeply, letting hope settle—rough but strong. Her eyes stung, but her lips curved into a small smile.

"People here keep their lives in perfect little boxes," she said softly, looking at a paint drip on her sketchbook.

She almost laughed, her voice quiet.

"Not everyone fits in the box, Sera. Some of us color outside the lines." She touched her thorned rose tattoo on her wrist, steadying herself.

She closed the sketchbook carefully, smoothing the bag so no pages would bend. She brushed hair from her eyes, ready to be fully herself no matter the test.

Standing tall, fingers brushing the soft leaves, she smelled the damp earth. She straightened her blouse, lifted her chin, her heart full of memories of struggle and strength. As she left her secret place, her resolve burned brighter—she would not let this world take away the wild, thorny beauty that made her unique.

Tension in the Boardroom

The boardroom is bright with morning light streaming through the glass walls. The city below looks small and distant. On the shiny table, reflections move—a quick ripple, a flick of hands, a frown illuminated by the bright lights. Olivia Barnes stands up, her suit neat against the black chairs and steel. Everyone falls silent. This room is about rules and order. Here, following the old ways is not just tradition but a means to avoid chaos.

Olivia speaks clearly, neither loud nor fast. "In my view, this change would hurt our brand. Drake Investment Empire isn't about one person's idea. We stand for stability—a reputation built over decades. What Ms. Hayes suggests," Olivia's green eyes scan the room carefully, "is creative but unproven. The board can't risk trying new things. Our owners expect us to be steady, not to shake things up."

The room feels tense, filled with the pressure of a meeting where careers hang in the balance. Olivia notices each notebook, each lowered gaze. Everyone here knows the rules: stay safe, protect your job, trust the system but not those who run it.

The company culture runs deep here. It's in the quiet hum of the air conditioning and the frosted glass showing traces of long-gone ambition. Decisions at Drake follow strict patterns. The top team—remembered through old names on a brass panel by the elevator—knows that taking risks can be seen as betrayal. Maintaining order is how they justify every promotion and every strict rule. A damaged reputation lasts for years. For Olivia, this is her duty: to protect the company and keep it strong.

She guards tradition. Personal ideas are rare and limited, and she has shaped herself to avoid surprises. In this room, one break from the norm can spread like a rumor, casting doubt after the doors close.

Seraphina listens, steady and ready. When Olivia stops, Seraphina stands, sunlight warming her figure and softening the sharp edges of the room.

"I disagree," she says calmly, her eyes bright. "Being real isn't a weakness. It's what sets us apart in a world where 'safe' feels dull. I believe in our brand and in growing it. We know how to lead. Sometimes leading means making new rules, not just following old ones. Our clients want something real, not something tested by a focus group. We should show that we can create, not just protect."

For a moment, the room feels less like a game and more like a test. The sunlight breaks into pieces on the faces watching closely. Seraphina's quiet defiance adds color to the room's gray routine. She demonstrates that control and creativity don't always conflict.

There's a whisper around the table. Peter, a man used to tracking results every few months, leans toward Gina and says quietly, "This isn't a design studio. If she wins, we'll look foolish." Gina shrugs slightly, her eyes moving between Seraphina and Olivia, trying to gauge the change.

Jasper Collins, usually quiet, nods slightly to Seraphina. This small support feels like rebellion here. Richard follows Olivia, arms folded, showing quiet disapproval, his jaw tight.

Caius Drake sits at the far end, still as a shadow. His eyes scan everyone. He says nothing—he rules a place that doesn't tolerate doubt, but something in his gaze flickers, mixing thought with feeling. Seraphina's words hit a nerve he tries to hide. For a moment, his power feels uncertain.

The silence grows—heavy with different emotions. Olivia holds her hands behind her back, finishing her points. People look quickly from Seraphina to Caius, caught between challenge and control, new ideas facing old rules.

For a while, only the soft sound of the city filters in. Freedom feels far beyond the glass. The meeting remains open—a moment of tension, waiting, where standing out could be costly.

The boardroom feels quiet as the meeting concludes. Sunlight shines on chrome and wood, creating patterns on the walls that seem to remember the argument. Seraphina remains seated at the far end. Others pick up papers and talk softly, trying to forget the confrontation. The smell of espresso and clean air mingles. Footsteps cross the marble floor—Gina's heels, Peter's slow steps—then fade as people leave one by one.

Seraphina straightens, her fingers brushing her sketchbook marked with a gray smudge. The debate still stings, but her voice remains strong. She breathes in the cool air and recalls warmth—the laughter at her mother's kitchen table and paint on old furniture. Even with doubts surrounding her, she doesn't soften.

"I trust this project," she says, her hand steady on the table's wood. "Being real isn't just a risk. It's how we stand out—how we create something that matters beyond quick profits."

Jasper smiles and nods to her—a quiet sign of support, soft as a brushstroke in a dark corner. But Seraphina's eyes pass over Richard's frown and Peter's doubt as if she's already prepared for them.

At the door, Olivia lingers, arms crossed, nails tapping. She watches Seraphina as if weighing a gem. Light glints off Olivia's watch. Her sharp eyes meet Marcus Langston's for a quick private conversation—low voices to avoid stirring the mood further.

"That kind of thinking won't last here," Olivia says quietly, polite but firm. "She's creative, yes, but she won't follow the rules. We can't risk the company for a bit of showmanship."

Marcus listens carefully. His eyes, marked by experience, observe Seraphina's strong stance and the fire within her.

"Give her a chance," he says calmly. "Sometimes change is the only way to discover what old ways can't."

Olivia tightens her arms. "Sometimes change breaks things we can't fix," she replies, her words trailing off as the door closes.

Caius sits at the far end, shaped by the sunlight hitting the glass wall. The city below is orderly, appearing indifferent to the tensions above. He stands, jaw tight, hands folded calmly on the table. When he speaks, the room listens, quiet and careful.

"We will consider all ideas," he says. "I understand the value of disagreement. This firm is built on questioning old ideas, even when it hurts. There will be more time to think. I expect you all to remain open."

His words bring silence—the room accepts that change, messy as it is, is sometimes necessary. The meeting concludes. Richard sighs, a chair scrapes, and then only Caius and Seraphina remain, standing on opposite sides of the polished room.

She leans back, watching the sunlight create moving patterns on the wall. She reflects on how she got here. This place, where even silence feels heavy, where every move counts, was not made for people like her. Her mother's voice echoes in her memory—stay strong, don't let them make you small. The memory fills the gaps left by cold looks and careful words.

She wonders if her stubbornness can crack this empire's surface. If behind all the rules, people like Caius might see that the company was made for real people, not just endless ambition. Maybe change can come slowly—one brave act, one refusal to settle.

She picks up her sketchbook and stands. She feels Caius's gaze—a flash of something unspoken, a question hanging between them. Their eyes meet for a brief moment, full of the things left unsaid. Outside, the city shines beyond the glass. The boardroom is still, holding its secrets and the shifting power within. Seraphina leaves, leaving Caius alone in light and shadow—waiting for the challenge only he can face.

The Orion Club Initiation

Late afternoon light shines cold across the twenty-eighth floor of the Drake Investment Empire Headquarters. Glass and steel rise above the city. The walls hold quiet secrets. In the design department, a low buzz fills the air—screen reflections flicker, keystrokes tap out pieces of important projects, and a quiet tension hums as if the building is holding its breath. Shadows grow longer on the smooth marble floor.

Suddenly, footsteps break the silence. Caius's aide, dressed perfectly in a sharp suit, walks with clear purpose. He moves through the desks as if he doesn't follow the usual office rules. People stop what they're doing, tense up, but don't look up. Seraphina watches from the corner of her eye, her hands poised over her graphic tablet. She's working on a campaign redesign, drawing a sunrise that doesn't match the bright, sterile room around her.

The aide stops by her desk, casting a shadow over her drawings. He doesn't say anything but hands her a heavy black envelope. The envelope is made from thick, dark paper that absorbs light. A silver pattern of the Orion constellation shines on it, and Caius Drake's neat signature is on the front. The envelope feels like it belongs to another world, a hidden network beneath the city's surface.

No one speaks. The busy office feels as if it's holding still. Seraphina takes the envelope—it's cold and heavy, almost as if it could hurt if handled roughly. When the aide leaves, everyone goes back to work, heads down, but she can feel quiet questions in the air. She shows no sign of curiosity, holding herself like steel under her denim jacket.

At her desk, she carefully opens the envelope without breaking the wax seal. Inside is a white card with a raised texture and shiny writing. It has her name—Seraphina Hayes—under a strong official crest. The card reads: Invitation to the Orion Club, Exclusive Event, Tonight. Keep it secret.

The card makes her heart beat fast. The Orion Club is a secret, powerful group in New York, filled with business leaders and people who control the city behind the scenes. It is not just a place but a symbol of power and influence. Getting invited means stepping into a world of silent control and hidden rules.

She remembers arguing with Caius in his private boardroom just an hour ago, their voices sharp and tense. Now, this invitation lies in her hands. Is it a test? A challenge? A warning wrapped in trust?

She reads "Discretion" again. The word feels heavy. She glances at Olivia Barnes, who furrows her brow as she briefly notices the envelope. In this office, where everything seems open and watched, true secrets are rare and valuable.

What will accepting this invitation cost her? She recalls Caius's calm but cold look, the way she refused to back down even when the room felt tight around her. Her defiance is clear, and now curiosity burns inside her like a small flame in a secret place.

She leans back, letting the blue light from her screen soften the edges of the card. The building runs on unspoken rules, older than its steel and glass. This is how empires keep control—not just with money, but with invitations and exclusions, each symbol like a secret code.

No one asks her what she received. The office follows unspoken rules strictly.

"Caius never invites people from our department," someone whispers softly.

"Maybe she's being moved," another says, with a mix of jealousy and fear.

Her jaw tightens.

"I'm still right here," she says with a small laugh, not letting rumors define her.

No one answers, and the tension fades.

She turns in her chair, both feet planted. The invitation in her hand glows softly, asking her to decide—go or stay back. She closes her eyes. The taste of coffee lingers on her tongue, reminding her of afternoons in her café, of art that accepts mistakes, and of laughter that isn't controlled by rules. Tonight, none of those comforts will be with her. But giving up is not an option. She slides the invitation into her worn bag with her sketches and pencils.

The office keeps working as dusk spreads across the windows. Seraphina stands, nerves tight, and slings her bag over one shoulder. Her unfinished design glows on the screen—a half-made horizon daring her to finish it later. She wonders what version of herself will return tomorrow.

She takes one last look—at her work, at the neat desks, at the world she will leave behind for one night. Then she moves, each step quiet but full of challenge, toward the fading light where day turns to night.

A taxi stops by the curb, splashing reflections into puddles near Seraphina's boots. She steps out, rain clinging to her coat, and looks at the huge hotel. Its pale stone looks old and cold, with no sign or name, except for the black envelope in her hand, cool with the silver star design. She stands still, breathing in the wet smell, then looks up at tall windows lit only by thin amber light inside. The doorway offers no welcome—just a heavy door with no name, as if the building itself hides secrets in its stone.

Her hands shake as she takes the invitation from her pocket. It feels important and heavy. She breathes deeply, hoping for warmth, but finds only rain and a fast heartbeat. She presses her lips together, remembering laughter at her café, friends' voices, and peaceful evenings. None of that is here—in this shadowy place.

The door opens not by her, but by a nod from two guards. They wear dark suits and serious faces. She hands them the card. Without a word, one guard steps aside, and the other gestures inside. Seraphina feels both watched and invisible, like a living work of art in a place made for neither. The air smells of polished wood and cigar smoke beneath heavy curtains.

A marble staircase appears, covered with a red carpet that swallows sound. Her heels make soft echoes as she walks down, each step both welcome and warning. To her left, old mirrors show her alone—chestnut hair, tight jaw, aware she doesn't belong here.

Past old portraits and soft lights, she reaches another checkpoint. More guards, sharper and less friendly, take her invitation, nod, and open tall wooden doors.

Inside, sound disappears. The air is thick and sharp like winter air. A quiet hum fills the room. The space is large, with dark wooden walls and warm light. Persian rugs soften her steps. Each pattern feels like a secret code she doesn't know yet. Many men in tuxedos stand in small groups, stiff and alert as if watched by invisible eyes. Their gazes pass over her, sizing her up, then return to old alliances.

Soft jazz music plays under quiet whispers. Here, people don't share news with friends but with careful allies. "You're taking risks, David." "Not yet. Not while they believe in the future." "Deals will happen. I won't miss out." Their words hint at market moves and power struggles. No one laughs. Hands hold glasses tightly as if trying to hide old wounds.

Seraphina stands tall. She moves like she is following lines she didn't draw, fingers brushing a curl behind her ear. No one speaks to her. Every smile feels sharp, and every look judges her. The walls seem to hold secrets, choosing silence over truth. The space between guests isn't connection but cold competition. Power is money; weakness is debt; friendships are just moves to be played.

This place is made to exclude. She wonders if any kindness or honesty can live in this cold place. She wants laughter, color, real joy, voices that speak just because they want to. The urge to run is strong, but she sets her jaw and walks deeper into the shadow-filled room. Fear isn't welcome, but curiosity pushes her forward.

At the edge of the crowd, a man moves—a sharp silhouette, separate but noticed. Caius stands among men who seem like statues, his silver tie pin shining with his every move. He breaks from the group and looks at Seraphina. She hopes for warmth but feels cold instead. His lips move for a quick, mechanical greeting.

"You're early," he says, his voice sharp.

"Tough traffic," she replies, with a dry smile.

His eyes glance to the bar, then back. He signals a waiter, who quickly comes and hands Seraphina a glass.

"For nerves or for show?" she asks, looking at the golden drink.

He raises an eyebrow. "They're watching."

"I noticed." She raises her glass, her eyes scanning the faces that refuse to see her as a person, searching for any weakness in the wall of masks.

His hand briefly touches her elbow, neither holding her back nor inviting her forward. Other guests return to their careful talks, a quiet wave pushing them away. Still looking at Caius, Seraphina drinks—her throat burning with both the drink and her own will.

He nods slightly, a hint of warning or praise, and gestures for her to follow. Together, they slip out of the lounge, leaving the cold games of the club behind for the secret halls ahead.

Caius walks ahead, his steps clear on the red carpet that winds through the Orion Club. The hallways are quiet and rich with dark wood panels under old lights, heavy picture frames holding serious portraits, and thick walls stopping the noise from outside. Soft curtains block the city sound, leaving only scent and secrets. They stop in a small space lit warmly and still, away from the crowd. He points to an old leather bench, worn smooth. Seraphina sits, feeling the weight of the quiet and memory.

Caius takes the seat opposite her, calm but sharp. He looks around, careful for listening ears or danger, then fixes his eyes on her, cold but controlled. His voice is clear and sharp. "The Orion Club is old," he says. "It stands because its members keep secrets. Loyalty isn't given; it's earned by trust—a value like money. Being part of this means working with others and also competing. You belong, or you have nothing."

The room feels tight, waiting to see her next move. She leans forward, tracing patterns on the bench. Her eyes narrow in the dim light. "Or you are free," she says quietly, heat in her voice. "What's the point of belonging when it's built on fear and secrets no one touches? You call it tradition. I see a wall built to keep out anything real or honest. You don't truly trust anyone. Yet you want loyalty from people who'd fight each other for power."

The air grows thick between them. Caius's jaw tightens—a small sign of doubt from a man who rarely shows it. The quiet traps their tension, the fight between caution and something raw and dangerous. "Trust must be controlled. There's no room for being naive. Success pulls in enemies. One mistake, and years of work fall apart." His gray eyes flash, cold but clear. "Compassion is a luxury here. You talk of honesty and strength as if they aren't weapons that will hurt you."

Seraphina sees a flash behind his mask—a weakness, a wish for gentleness hidden by caution. She pushes. "You talk like you're always hunted. Maybe you are. But don't you ever wonder what it would be like to let someone in? To risk a little, just to feel something real, not just control?"

Her voice shakes a bit but stays strong. The room feels like it's closing in.

Caius's reply is sharper, cutting the air. "Control isn't protection. It's the only way to stop chaos. Without it, there's no empire—only ruin." His hand grips his glass tightly—crystal against hard flesh. "What you call kindness, I call weakness. I can't afford weakness."

"Maybe that's why you're alone," she says softly but boldly, holding his gaze. The words hang heavy, daring the room to react. "You have all these men bowing to the idea of power, but none would bleed for you. They'd watch you fall and take your place."

He doesn't look away. "And what do you want me to do? Risk everything on hope? Let feelings decide the fate of the club, the company, my family? That's not leadership. That's a dream."

Their voices rise, sharp and heated.

"You think honesty is weakness?"

"I think it gives your enemies power."

"You think fear keeps you safe?"

"I know it keeps enemies cautious."

"You lead with fear and wonder why you feel nothing!"

"And you think trust costs nothing until you lose everything!"

"At least I believe in something more than survival!"

"Survival is the only real win."

A sudden, quiet pause, sharp and fragile. Their anger and truth are shown clearly, past hurts and hidden hopes visible beneath. Caius loosens his grip on the glass. Seraphina looks for a crack, a sign he might give in. But they both sit straight, not ready to give up. Still, something has changed. The soft noise from the club comes back as the quiet fades, and for a moment, Caius and Seraphina sit in stillness—altered, but still guarded.

Fires Beneath the Surface

Seraphina's footsteps echoed across the marble floor of the Drake Investment Empire lobby, breaking the quiet stillness. This place was cold and empty, with glass walls and dark corners. The city stretched out beyond the windows, bright lights shining through the night. Caius sat behind his desk, sharp and exact in his suit, calm and unreadable.

She entered without knocking, her anger pressing against the cold calm of the office. The door clicked shut behind her. The room smelled faintly of metal and electronics. Her hands buzzed with nervous energy as she steadied herself after feeling shut out.

"You made the choice on the Stonebridge project," she said sharply. "You didn't even consider my team's work or my advice."

Caius looked up calmly. His gray eyes were sharp and steady. His desk was neat, with only a folder and a small metal sculpture on it. He remained calm.

"The Stonebridge move needed a focused plan. Bringing everything together is what keeps investors confident. Taking extra risks wasn't logical." His voice was measured and firm, ending the argument before it could start.

Seraphina caught a slight crack in his calm—just for a moment. She moved across the floor to stand in front of the large window. Outside, the city buildings glowed gold and blue. Inside, she stood out, her bright energy breaking the gray stillness. The city didn't care about their fight; it just carried on.

"Extra risk?" she challenged. "It was new ideas. You want the future to fit into your neat little rules, but creativity doesn't. You can't build tomorrow by only holding on to the past."

Caius's eyes narrowed. He stood up slowly, carefully, like a chess player preparing for his move. "Miss Hayes, rules exist for a reason. Personal goals, without control, can ruin what this company has built." His voice was sharp now, but his jaw tightened, revealing a moment of doubt.

Their voices rose, both refusing to back down.

"You speak of rules, but you never asked why we suggested this plan. It's not about ego. It's about doing better work. Just once, admit that someone outside your close circle might see something you don't."

"I admit nothing like that. Leadership isn't a democracy."

"Then it's not leadership; it's pride." The word hung heavy between them.

He didn't respond immediately, as she expected. Instead, a quiet tension filled the room, as if the city itself leaned in. For a brief moment, his carefully built mask slipped, revealing a hidden vulnerability. Seraphina realized that weakness doesn't just go against power—it's where light or destruction can get in.

Inside, Seraphina felt a mix of heat and fear. Every protest was both a defense of her team and her place in a harsh business world where creativity is only welcome if it makes money. Behind her words, courage mixed with fear—the fear of being erased, of becoming just another forgotten piece in the system. She couldn't show this fear, but every heartbeat cried out: she had to win, not for pride, but to prove she couldn't be erased.

Caius also felt shaky beneath his calm. Where he wanted respect, Seraphina offered honesty and fire. She was an unexpected force: neither begging nor equal, but someone who refused to be controlled. The old rules of power faltered when faced with someone who stopped playing by them. What was left if he couldn't move her?

They stood, two silhouettes against the city sky—worlds built for distance suddenly close in breath, shadow, and shared tension. Their eyes locked in a silent challenge neither fully understood. For a moment, they were just two uncertain people, the clash of their worlds filled with fear of what might survive.

Night pressed against the windows of Seraphina's Café. The city's distant sounds were soft beneath music playing from hidden speakers. The door opened to cool air; Seraphina came in, her coat tight around her, still shaking from the fight she left behind in the glass tower. Inside, warm light spilled over brick walls and wood, shining on scattered sketches and mugs. Jasper waited, two hot coffees in front of him, his smile a mix of welcome and concern.

Seraphina slumped into a worn armchair, exhaustion heavy on her shoulders. Her hands wrapped around the mug he handed her, the warmth soothing the tingle left by adrenaline. The bitter espresso mixed with cinnamon and sugar was familiar and comforting. Around them, the café held its quiet, fairy lights flickering softly against the street noise.

Jasper didn't ask questions—he just waited, letting silence give her room to speak until she tightened her grip and her voice cracked.

"It's like talking to a wall of glass and steel. He just—" She could still see the city lights through Caius's figure, hear his cold, sharp words. "I gave every reason. Every fact. He acted like none of it mattered. Like *I* didn't matter. I'm exhausted, Jasper. There's no breath in that place, just power games and perfect surfaces. I can't breathe there."

He listened, chin in hand, eyes focused on her as the world fell away. Her frustration spilled out—her doubts and anger pressing tight inside. In her mind, the fight replayed: her voice rising, refusing to give in. Caius's cold stare lingered too, and under her anger was a pain she didn't want to face. Am I just a piece on their board? Will I lose myself if I keep fighting in a place that won't see me?

"Remember that mural job last fall?" Jasper said softly, steady as the floorboards. "Half the building board wanted to cancel it, saying it 'wasn't what fancy tenants wanted.' You painted it anyway. Now people line up for pictures with your art." His smile was kind but firm. "You don't let anyone push you around. Not the city, not some billionaire with a big ego. Don't let him shrink you. He doesn't get to decide who you are."

"You say that," she said softly, feeling some of the weight lift, "but this is different. It's not just spray paint on a wall. It's a giant machine of rules and secret deals. Sometimes, I'm afraid I'll just... bend, little by little." She traced the rose tattoo on her wrist, touching the inked thorns. She saw herself swallowed by glass hallways and meetings until all that was left was compromise. Does she have the strength to stay true, or will Caius's cold gaze wear her down?

Jasper reached across the table, covering her hand with his. "Hey. You made this place," he said, sweeping his arm across the mismatched chairs and art-covered walls, "with scraps and vision. You fought for every part." His voice was gentle—"I know you want to do good work, but you don't have to lose yourself to do it. Caius might be strong, but so are you. You choose to build, not break."

She snorted softly, a faint smile starting. Jasper's faith steadied her, grounding her in something real beyond the office fights—reminding her she wasn't alone. Under the candlelight, her tired strength began to heal.

He leaned closer, his voice soft over the music. "Just... be careful, okay? People like Caius? They're storms. I see how you look at him—it's not just business. Getting close means you might get caught in the storm. And it's hard to find your way back."

She laughed, shaking her hair away. "Thanks for the drama, Jasp." But she felt his worry behind the words, the worry of someone who had fixed her before. "You're right. I just... I don't want to lose myself. Not for a job. Not for anyone." The tightness in her chest eased, replaced by firm resolve.

They stood, the chairs creaking beneath them, and Seraphina hugged Jasper tightly, grateful. The smell of coffee and old books clung to him, keeping her grounded. Outside, streetlights turned the sidewalk gold, the city quiet. As she stepped back into the night, warmth from the café following her, Seraphina stood tall. Tomorrow, the fight continues. Tonight, she is steady—strong beneath a human skin.

The air was cold the moment Caius entered the penthouse. The lights turned on smoothly. He took off his jacket, letting it drop onto a marble bench that reflected the room's cold feel. The silence here was firm, broken only by the soft hum of the city beyond the glass.

His shoes tapped on the polished floor that mirrored his movements in pale shapes. He walked past steel sculptures and sharp art toward the wall of windows, drawn to the city—alive, unstoppable, uncaring.

He breathed in deeply, his jaw tightening as he pressed his fists together. The memory of the evening's fight echoed in his mind: Seraphina's bright, honest voice refusing to give in. Her words still floated in the air, bitter and sharp. He had managed power plays and crises with ease, but she had entered the storm with only conviction, breaking his rhythm.

He paced by the glass wall. New York stretched below, a network of lights and busy windows full of life. He tried to replay the conversation in his mind—each piece of language, each sharp look from her eyes. Her refusal to submit had sharp edges, making cracks in his control. Instead of falling under his power, Seraphina challenged it. Her strong presence still sparked along his nerves, disrupting him. Control, he realized, was more fragile than he thought. The air tasted sharp and hopeful—a sign of something new.

He poured whiskey into a glass, the amber liquid catching the city's light. The smell mixed sharp oak and smoke, a small comfort. He turned the glass in his hand, noticing his face reflected in the window: pale, sharp, eyes tired from holding control. A faint scar above his left eyebrow marked his skin—a small sign he rarely saw. It reminded him of a night of betrayal—the night that taught him to never trust without thinking. That scar was the line holding his mask in place—a warning to give up only what was needed.

But tonight, something shifted. Seraphina's defiance stayed with him and unsettled him. He remembered her small, ink-stained hands, alive with meaning, as she made her points. She had looked at him—not afraid or in awe, but with fire. For years, his world had been built on clear logic and control. Her presence threatened it. She saw through the act, naming the need for order as a kind of hurt, as if she understood the cost. Could she?

Caius sat on the edge of a gray couch, cool beneath his palms. Neon lights danced in his glass; the city's reflection broke into golden bits. He tried to find the certainty that always guided him—to remind himself who he was: a man who shaped cities, whose will survived every betrayal. Instead, he felt haunted by the thought that power felt emptier than before. The room was quiet, soft as dusk on stone. His heart beat fast with conflict: hunger for control and a reckless flicker of hope. Somehow, Seraphina saw him—no rival, partner, or teacher ever had.

If she could break his walls, what else might change? He rubbed the scar on his brow, feeling the memory of pain and shame—the lesson that trust can kill. Years of planning every move, weighing every word, hiding every weakness—but now, in the echo of her voice, in the spark of her honest, defiant spirit, he wanted something new: truth, risk, fragile hope. The idea scared him, making his skin feel thin under his armor.

He stood, restless again, and went to the windows—his silent guards, keeping the world out. The city glowed, cold and huge, offering no answers. For a moment, he imagined lowering his defenses, speaking honestly instead of playing games—what would be left? Who would he be without his mask?

He pressed his hand to the glass, matching his heartbeat to the city's steady rhythm. Power had always been his refuge, rules his shield. But after Seraphina's rebellion, he felt exposed—curious and scared of the future she opened. He couldn't stop thinking about her shadow in his mind. For the first time in years, hope and fear twisted together and looked the same.

He stood still, spine tight, staring at the city's lights as if they held answers. The penthouse was a fortress, but tonight it felt less safe and more like a cage he built himself, afraid of what would happen if he let go, even for a moment.

Secrets and Shadows

Bright noon light reflects off the glass walls of the Drake Investment building, giving the marble lobby a shiny appearance as Evelyn Drake steps inside. The air smells faintly of metal, sharp and tense—a place meant to impress and keep even old-money families in line. Evelyn remains calm. Her heels click softly on the floor, making junior employees glance up from their phones. Security guards watch her closely. She quickly shows her keycard, a sign of her authority, and the doors open without fuss.

The elevator takes her up. The mirrors break her reflection into pieces—neat hair, a clean navy suit, a pale hand holding a leather bag. Her heart beats faster as she remembers a cold argument years ago with Caius in a glass hallway, his harsh words like cold breath, her replies filled with pain she can't take back. Old memories hang here, frozen in time.

She walks down the hall to Caius's office, the place where he quietly runs his empire. Marcus Langston and Seraphina Hayes emerge from a meeting, their faces serious. Evelyn notices Seraphina, who feels out of place like a bright splash of color on a gray wall. Seraphina looks away nervously. Marcus just nods, careful and protective.

The office is neat and cold—big windows create sharp shadows across metal and dark stone. Evelyn closes the door softly, placing her bag down carefully, reclaiming a space she's long missed.

Caius looks tense, his voice short. "This isn't a good time, Evelyn."

"I find you're never available, even for your own building," Evelyn replies. She looks at the metal art on the wall, sharp and abstract, shining in the sunlight. Her face is calm, but her jaw is tight, filled with old anger.

"You could have made an appointment with my assistant."

"And been brushed off or ignored again?" She now looks him straight in the eyes, standing partly in shadow among wires and steel. "Your messages go unanswered. Your calls are 'lost.' I wonder—is it business that's too hard for you, or is it our family?"

"I have duties here. The trust is managed by rules, not by mood."

Evelyn notices a glimpse of the brother she once knew, the cold act covering tiredness or painful memories neither wants to admit. "Honesty would serve you better, Caius. Our family legacy isn't a game to be swept away when it suits you."

He narrows his eyes. "If you want a confession, you're in the wrong place."

"How fitting." Her laugh is quiet and bitter. "You always wanted your truth clean and quiet." She touches one sharp metal sculpture—it shines like the family trust their parents left them, meant to hold them together but instead binding them with unspoken rules. She recalls another office, another fight: sharp words, broken promises, her mother's tears; a secret kept by one sibling, hated by the other. That division never healed, only covered up by polite distance.

Outside, Marcus stands stiffly in the hall, surrounded by nervous junior workers. He pretends to focus on his phone, but his posture is ready to stop trouble. Seraphina's worried eyes move from door to door. Everyone here knows what happens when family fights go public—whispers spread and break the calm like a cold wind.

Evelyn lowers her voice until it's almost a whisper. "The family is uneasy, Caius. Your recent changes have worried more than just me. The trust isn't your private safe. There are consequences when you treat legacy like power rather than responsibility."

Caius replies coldly, "If the board has problems, they follow the rules. What consequences, Evelyn? Are we threatening each other now?"

"Think of it as a warning. Ignore us, and you'll see what a family in revolt can do. Your name on this building doesn't make you untouchable." She moves closer, as if her nearness could force honesty, her determination shaped by years of standing up to him.

He says nothing, his jaw tight, fingers gripping the desk. Old wounds fill the room, mixed with the smell of metal and old papers—betrayal as if it were alive. A scar flashes under the light on his forehead.

She stops at the door, framed by morning light and power. "Expect more, Caius. From me—and from all of us." Her heels click once, twice, then she walks away, leaving Caius alone in the glass fortress, fists clenched, watching the city below.

Seraphina stops at the gallery entrance, her shoes silent on pale marble. Afternoon light shines through tall windows, creating patterns between the blank walls and paintings. The room is quiet except for the city hum far below and the soft sound of footsteps above. She breathes out, feeling the tension from the upper floors fade, replaced by the smell of paint. The silence feels fragile, like the calm after a storm she didn't see but can almost feel.

Paintings hang sparsely on white walls. One shines with blue and gold streaks. She reaches out but doesn't touch, imagining the artist's hand, sure then unsure, bold then hesitant. Her mind drifts back to Caius earlier: his cold jaw, the way he cut off her design idea, his quick dismissal. That memory stings, but here among the quiet art, her anger softens. She had seen him recently, his hand trembling briefly before hiding it under papers—hidden, but not gone.

She walks past steel sculptures, their shadows sharp and wild. The gallery window shows another city view, soft and golden, unlike the hard, cold glass upstairs. She finds a bench near a bronze sculpture shaped like a snake. Sitting down, she hugs her knees, trying to calm the storm inside.

Her mind flashes to the last fight with Caius—her sharp voice, his cold answers, the hard look in his eyes. But then she remembers a different scene: late night in empty offices, blue city light through windows. Caius hunched over his desk, chair turned away from the city, head in hands. She saw this through a crack in the door, like a ghost caught between moments. The glow from his screen showed his tense shoulders and small breath shakes. No harsh words then, just silence—heavy and full. This image unsettles her. It felt human, a break in his tough armor that made her heart tilt.

She takes out her worn sketchbook and draws jagged lines, sharp and tangled like her thoughts. It's easier to draw than to understand her feelings. She thinks about the moment she saw his eyes glaze over when he thought no one noticed, the quiet sigh, a rare sign of regret in his strong front. She wonders how many stresses weigh on him—business, family, the loneliness of power. Are her harsh words any different from the ones he keeps inside?

She imagines something surprising and risky—that behind the empire's cold rules and wealth, he's just a fragile man, like an artist shaping clay. She wonders what it would be like to look past the CEO, to see the son, brother, and man who quietly grieves. What if she could stop judging and start understanding? The idea is both hopeful and scary.

Her hand steadies, drawing softer, slower lines. She closes the book with a soft snap—a quiet promise inside. She's tired of battles based on half-truths. She tells herself to pay close attention, listen between words, and try to see what's behind the strong show of ambition and mistakes. Compassion is risky, like walking a tightrope on glass towers, but maybe that's what they both need.

Seraphina stands, smoothing her skirt and looking once more at the sculpture. She steps into the hall, standing taller, chin up. The corridor hums with faint echoes of raised voices down the stairs. A new promise lives in her chest: to see, to seek, to soften. She disappears into the quiet, her resolve quietly growing.

The boardroom hums with recycled air and distant city noise. Screens glow cold light; numbers change on dark wood and glass. Marcus sits across from Caius, his tablet showing coded files. He leans forward, stubble dusting his face in the bright light, and says, "These numbers. Residential real estate investment trusts—REITs—started acting strangely three days ago. We found quick trades moving money out from our main accounts. No approved deals match this." He shows the tablet to Caius, who quietly studies the falling returns. "Fifteen million moved overnight," Marcus says quietly. "The system flagged problems, then—" He stops, his jaw tight. "Pierce's company is on the other end, using risky, complicated options. Damien is betting the market will change soon."

Caius's face is steady but serious. He doesn't answer right away. His mind lists the board members—family, rivals, allies—each a threat or key player. The empire feels sharp and dangerous tonight. "Any leaks inside?" he asks, his voice calm. Marcus shakes his head, but not fully sure. "No weaknesses found yet."

The halls buzz with low nervous energy from people who sense change is coming. Caius walks down marble and glass floors, the executive wing flowing like a vein running slow now. Voices rise in a glass meeting room—two department heads argue loudly.

"You said clients were safe!"

"They were—until someone let Pierce undercut us—"

"I didn't leak anything! Maybe check with—"

Caius's presence stops the fight. Both turn to him, silence snapping quickly.

He moves on, mirrors in the doors reflecting him. Near marketing, stress sounds heavy—words like "fallout," "exposure," and "pivot" float then fade. Workers shrink when he enters. Conversations drop to whispers so quiet the floor seems to swallow them. Fake orchid smells fill the air, trying to replace something natural that won't survive here.

Under all the glass and marble, the heart of Drake Investment beats with warning. Clean surfaces and neat order show strength, but the air can't hide the quiet smell of fear. Light softens into blue as dusk gathers outside giant windows, hunting for weaknesses built into the city.

Seraphina works in a small white design office lit by humming LEDs. Her fingers draw lines on a digital tablet, thinking of colors and textures. She's alone, but outside, voices trail by:

"They're not saying layoffs, but no one knows…"

"Pierce is up to something. Did you see the derivatives report?"

"Don't send that file. He'll notice."

She checks her phone and texts:

Jasper. Things are serious. People are worried. Layoffs?

Across the street, Jasper sits in her favorite café, the city blurring behind him. He reads and replies:

Pretty sure they just like to scare people. If you see me looking for jobs online tomorrow, stand up for me, okay?

His jokes hide his nerves—he taps the table, eyes on the door every few seconds.

She answers:

Not funny. Seriously. I've never seen this before.

Her heart beats faster as texts flash. The usual struggles feel different now, edged with a cold taste of fear. Anxiety spreads from server rooms through clean halls, lots of small, tense clicks from those too proud to admit they're scared.

In his office, Caius stands before the glass—like a giant fighting his own doubts. The skyline glows with circuits and sunset, a city alive and uncaring. His reflection looks down—a perfect suit, but his jacket shows stress, and a pale scar shines above his eye.

He thinks: Who is on my side? Who's just looking out for themselves? Marcus stays calm, but even the strongest rock breaks under pressure. If he keeps secrets—or anyone does—even this stronghold will crack.

No one teaches you how to lead something too big to control. Even the strongest glass breaks under stress. Tonight, the empire shining over the city feels fragile as spun sugar.

Caius tightens his tie. Below, the streets roar on—blind, hungry, careless. The city doesn't care about empires or the men who build them, only about hunger, movement, and power that shifts. He looks over the lights, searching for answers hidden behind the glass and neon.

Somewhere inside this order, chaos has begun.

The Art of Resistance

Sunlight shines through the large café windows, casting soft golden patterns on tables that have seen many stories and spilled sugar over the years. The smell of coffee and cinnamon fills Seraphina's Café, waking up even the tired first customers who come in from the quiet morning streets. The walls are made of exposed brick, decorated with pieces of canvas and small potted plants. Seraphina moves quickly between the tables. She greets customers warmly and naturally, smiling at an old man's joke about the weather, then suggesting he try the cranberry scone. Near the window, a woman drawing in a worn notebook receives a free shot of espresso and a quiet nod from Seraphina, sharing a moment of artistic understanding. Outside, the soft city sounds come through the glass, but inside, time feels calm and comforting.

Seraphina moves easily from one regular customer to the next, laughter flowing as freely as the dark coffee and flaky croissants. She taps on the pastry case, refills mugs, and brushes her hand over the rough pot of a plant—all actions done without thinking, a well-practiced dance. Music from an acoustic guitar mixes with the sounds of plates and the light fluttering of a curtain, while an early heatwave stirs the world outside. Her café life is calm and changing, but it is grounded in care: Jasper texts her a joke about "caffeine magic," and Mrs. Padmore asks for her usual drink, extra honey included, even as Seraphina writes a list of things she needs to order. Her mornings are filled with laughter and notes stained with paint, her day shaped by the warmth of bread ovens and the feeling of belonging.

When the busy time slows down, Seraphina feels the quiet weight of routine around her. She wipes her wrist, where a rose tattoo with thorns peeks out from her sleeve, and pulls out her phone. She scrolls past missed calls from unknown numbers to find three urgent emails from Drake Investment Empire. Her thumb hesitates before giving a tired sigh, sinking into the pressure between the two parts of her life shown on her calendar.

She brings her notebook closer and sketches two logo ideas using the phone's light. A bold, colorful, and unusual idea spreads over the edge of a napkin. Her tablet hums as she creates a bright line of color, mixing curiosity with strong determination. Between refills and receipts, she escapes briefly into another world—one where ideas are measured like money and creativity is a risky, powerful force controlled by business plans and suits. Her email inbox warns her to "standardize creativity," reminding her that profit and invention don't always mix easily.

Her face tightens as she answers a question about almond milk, while a digital marketing campaign draft flickers in the back of her mind. Even here, in her cozy café with mismatched chairs and fairy lights, the outside world—aggressive and nonstop—is pressing in around her.

At noon, the kitchen smells heavy with flour and caramel. Seraphina takes off her apron, dusting flour from her hands. She closes the back door, trading the quiet hum of the espresso machine for the noisy city. On the phone, her voice softens as her mother's words come through—a gentle reminder about home. They talk about details, her mother's voice proud but worried, walking the line between support and concern for the world her daughter must face now.

In the busy streets, Seraphina isn't sheltered like she is in the café. Everything here feels rough: screeching subway brakes, perfume clinging to strangers' coats, tall buildings breaking sunlight into cold beams. The city demands action, not welcomes. She walks with purpose, shoulders tight, leaving warmth behind and heading into glass and steel. There is no room for hesitation where she is going.

Drake Investment Empire's headquarters rise tall, casting a long shadow over Wall Street. The lobby gleams under bright lights, filled with the sharp clicks of polished shoes and formal greetings. Security cameras blink as Seraphina swipes her card—every step controlled and recorded. The lobby is clean and empty of comfort—all angles sharp and challenging. In the elevator, she sees many reflections: messy hair controlled, café warmth hidden beneath professional black clothes. The change is complete.

The design room feels cold and simple, with desks like islands in a sea of black and white. Her area is crowded with forms and screens full of numbers, not faces. She checks briefs, edits digital drafts, and handles many Slack messages from marketing and design teams while her phone buzzes with reminders. Coworkers circle, looking for the confidence she wears like armor. Here, creativity feels broken down, made dull by meetings and expectations. There is no softness, only the dry taste of recycled air and pressure.

Seraphina sits under harsh lights, her fingers still stained with charcoal from earlier. Her eyes scan a large board where colors fight against the room's grayness. Soon, sharp-suited colleagues approach, their voices tense with expectation. She takes a deep breath, ready for the clash between her ideas and their authority. Her café self is hidden under polished professionalism, determined to protect the colors she believes in, even in a city that wants everything gray.

Amber light shines through the tall glass walls, catching a city caught between a busy day and a quiet evening. The conference room at Drake Investment Empire is perfectly neat, with a shiny black table, abstract metal artworks on white walls, and silent digital screens showing draft ads. The bright colors on the screens—red, blue, yellow—draw eyes away from the safe grays preferred by tradition.

Olivia Barnes stands at the head of the table, posture rigid, tablet in one hand and stylus in the other like a conductor's baton. The sharp edges of her jacket catch the light, and her green eyes study every design with cool judgment. Her fingers tap a touchpad. The main screen shows Seraphina's design: bright arcs of color, a smiling model holding a cup of black coffee, and the city outside blurred into hopeful shapes.

Her voice is clear and firm, just above the sound of the air system. "I'll be honest. These colors are almost too bright for a company like ours. The message is—what's the word? Unusual. This could damage the strong, traditional image we've built." Team members quickly take notes, pens moving nervously on papers. Every eye watches the back-and-forth between the two women, but the real watchers are the reflections in the shiny surfaces, seeing alliances form and break in seconds.

The tension feels hard and sharp. It fills the room like static in the air or footsteps on marble floors. Seraphina stands up, her back straight, breathing quietly in her own ears. The warmth of the café still clings to her skin, a hint of cinnamon and espresso under her blazer—out of place here. She notices the junior designers along the table, their pens tapping nervously, one wiping sweat from their brow. They seem curious, maybe supportive, but mostly unsure, caught in the pull of power and the fear of speaking up.

"I understand the history you want to protect," Seraphina says softly but clearly, careful not to raise her voice just to be loud. "But people outside recognize realness when they see it. These are not just colors or pretty pictures. This palette is more than a trend—it feels warm, trustworthy, and friendly. It's what people want from the ones who manage their money." She points to a panel showing client feedback: words like "unexpected but honest," "memorable," "finally human." "Recent surveys with clients and our own employee engagement show people want connection. The industry has changed. The old, boring corporate blue makes us invisible. I think we should risk standing out."

Her words fall like small stones into still water—spreading gently but slow to shake the hard center.

Olivia's face tightens as she switches screens. "You talk about market trends and what customers want, but you miss the core of our business. Investment work isn't for playful art. It's about stability, trust, and clear, familiar visuals. I'm telling you to tone down these colors. Use neutral tones and balanced fonts. Redo it by this afternoon."

Seraphina's heart pounds in her fingers. The old fear flares briefly—fear that this place will always close down ideas, that creativity is just decoration or a waste. But she steadies herself in the quiet, remembering late nights coloring posters at home, her mother's words telling her not to shrink back from power, and jobs that expected her to be small. She fought for the right to add bright color to a dull world; she won't give up here for a company that would forget her eyes' color tomorrow unless she made herself unforgettable.

She says, "My work is based on years of working with real clients—not just theory or style. These campaigns connect because they have life. We can fake safety, or we can be a rare place that feels real. I can make technical changes, but I won't erase what makes this important. I believe being real will keep us relevant long after another boring bank ad disappears."

The designers exchange looks—relief, worry, even respect passes like fresh air after rain. Tradition almost smothers the room, but something else stirs beneath: the chance for change, or at least the courage to try.

The room feels fragile, like glass ready to break. Olivia's lips press thin. She glances slightly at the senior partner beside her, who watches silently. Seraphina gathers her notes and tablet with steady hands.

Chairs scrape as people move. Olivia stays at the table's end, speaking quietly now, her words private and powerful. Seraphina leaves, the glass door closing on the clash of old and new, certainty and hope—leaving the air full of questions still waiting for answers.

Caius stands just outside the glass conference room, hands behind his back, his presence quiet beneath his sharp suit. The walls reflect a precise world—metal art, clean lines, light shining off cold marble. Inside, Seraphina stands straight as Olivia's sharp voice cuts through the quiet air.

She doesn't falter. Her posture is calm and sure, chin held high as she meets criticism head-on. Olivia's words are clinical—market survival, tradition, the company's public image as armor. Seraphina's answers are clear but not rebellious, focused on truth as a form of art. Her hands draw a calm curve in the air, explaining the colors, their meaning, and a vision that brings life to the dull world of finance.

A part of Caius—an old version of himself—sees the usual drill. This is a test; this place has always demanded obedience, not new ideas. But as he watches Seraphina, something new stirs—uncertain but sharp. There is tension: Olivia demands sameness; Seraphina refuses to let creativity be drowned by tradition. The junior designers watch nervously but with hope that something different might survive here.

He notices her calmness, the strong foundation under her clear replies. In this moment, she's not just defending art—she's claiming a place in a world built to resist change. Caius feels the contrast deep inside: the fortress he built in this empire, the myth of control, and the rare, refreshing challenge that someone might expose it as empty.

Minutes later, Seraphina stands at his office door, which closes softly behind her. This place is another world, full of power. Windows let in sunlight to dark corners; the sleek black desk marks the line between control and challenge. Caius sits straight, searching her face for cracks. She holds his gaze.

"I reviewed your proposal," he says quietly, each word heavy as if weighing the city. "It's... unusual. The board expects steady continuity—a brand built over many years. Help me understand what you want to do with such a different approach."

A tense silence follows. Seraphina answers calmly:

"The world outside has changed. People want honesty—they see through fake quickly. If we only give them what's safe and familiar, we'll be lost in the noise. I wanted to design something that feels like a real conversation, not a one-way message. The colors are meant to disrupt but also welcome. I used feedback from real clients—not just marketing talk but actual people. It's honesty that wins loyalty, not sameness."

The room holds its breath. Caius looks at her—her straight jaw, her quiet confidence, even as doubt hangs between them. He feels the weight of his own past—the strict discipline, the pain of betrayal. Control was safety. Now, in her words and bold vision, he senses that risking something may be better than holding on too tight.

He almost wants to question her more, to find a flaw. Instead, he leans forward, elbows on the desk. His doubt fades, replaced by a quiet respect. He realizes her honesty is not recklessness but strong will. In a cautious world, her bravery is a quiet rebellion he admires.

"I respect your honesty," he says, his voice softer now. "Too many here mistake not caring for being professional. Your designs have made the right people rethink things—even me."

Caius feels the grip of power loosen for a moment, replaced by the unfamiliar buzz of possibility. He knows change is a force that can't be stopped once it starts. What if the company—and he himself—adapted instead of resisted? Could the empire last if it moved forward, not against the future? There is risk in letting go. But also a clear cost in staying the same: a legacy worth nothing but empty marble halls, untouched by true innovation.

Seraphina stands steady, noticing the shift in his voice. She nods, tired but glowing with hope, strong but not defeated. Between them, a quiet understanding forms: they have seen each other more clearly, past their armor.

Caius nods back—small, unusual, but full of meaning. As Seraphina leaves, the hallway is silent, the sharp city air mixing with the filtered office atmosphere. She carries with her more than just defended ideas—she has earned respect, a rare and powerful thing here.

Lines Drawn

Night has quieted the city below, and the sky is a dull mix of gray and faint lights. Inside the Drake Investment Empire Headquarters, the large lobby is silent. The shiny marble floors reflect the light and Seraphina's figure as she walks, her shoulders squared against the cold air. Her boots echo in the stillness. Simple black leather benches and modern metal sculptures fill the space—a world of steel and order, controlled by the man waiting upstairs.

She reaches the elevator's steel doors and scans her ID card. The green light indicates her access is approved, and the doors open quietly. Inside, her face looks sharp and stretched in the shiny walls. The elevator rises through empty floors toward the top.

On the top floor, the air smells clean and sharp, with hints of lemon from constant cleaning. Her footsteps sound alone as she walks to the glass-walled conference room. The city lights spread out below like a grid of tiny stars. Caius sits at the far end of the long table. The bright light from a large LED panel highlights his sharp face and dark gray suit. Papers are stacked near his hands, and his eyes flicker with the blue light from multiple screens as he studies numbers.

He does not greet her, only nods shortly. "You're late."

"Only if you're counting disaster time," Seraphina replies, putting her bag on a chair and spreading out her sketches. She watches him carefully, looking for any sign of weakness.

Caius speaks clearly. "Your color choices won't work past the second slide. The gradient looks messy; investors won't understand the meaning." He looks at her, cold and focused.

"It's meant to feel real, not perfect," she answers. "We agreed this project needs feeling, not just neat numbers."

He slides a paper across to her. "Feeling can't be measured. The board trusts what can be measured. This isn't an art show."

She leans in, firm. "If you want the brand to matter in three years, people have to feel something. Otherwise, it's just another forgettable box."

"What you want can't be scaled. You want a gallery; we want control." He stays calm, his words sharp and clear.

Seraphina narrows her eyes. "Control is fake when your audience can swipe away and forget your billion-dollar legacy. If that scares you, then—"

He stops her, his voice cold. "If you want to shock, it's working."

She matches his tone. "If you want to kill anything real, you're succeeding."

Tension fills the room. The city behind him shines, uncaring, as if concrete gods expect these fights every night.

He looks down. "We'll keep your design. But the call to action must be clearer." He sends a note to her screen with some frustration. "Don't argue with me on readability."

She types quickly, not looking at him. "Don't argue with me on relevance."

They fall silent again. The tapping of keys, the soft hum of devices—and occasionally brief notes exchanged: a lighter line on a graph, a question about tone. They both make changes, accepting each other's corrections. She changes the banner; he fixes the data. Midnight nears, their conflict slowly fading.

He surprises her by finishing a half-done sketch with neat, useful labels—showing skill with visuals. She glances at him, noticing a small softening of his usual stern look. In the soft light, he seems less untouchable.

She stands, stretches, and goes to pour two coffees. The bitter smell fills the clean air. Caius looks over her new layout, now thoughtful, not negative.

They hold each other's gaze longer, curiosity growing into a wary, electric feeling. Not a truce, but a change: their friction sparking a new kind of connection.

When Seraphina looks across the glass table, midnight presses on the windows, and the city's map watches silently. Her heart skips. Caius's tired, empty look meets hers quietly.

She realizes she works with him, not against him. His cracks show not just resistance, but possibility. Beneath her defenses, something softer grows—a shared stubbornness, need, and fear of being overlooked or changed.

She wonders, tired and buzzing, who they are outside this fortress—if he sees her not just as a worker or rival, but as someone who won't disappear. Fatigue makes everything softer: easier to feel the pull between them, even as they try to break it.

For now, it stays unspoken, hanging quietly between demands. The moment stretches, warm and endless, promising both conflict and hope.

Seraphina comes back the next night, carrying bright printouts smelling of ink and possibility. The conference room glows with LED light pushing back the night through the glass. Caius stands by the window, his shadow broken by the glittering city below. The sky is dark blue and black, not quite giving up the night. The room feels removed from the busy world outside.

He doesn't turn as she enters. Numbers flash on the tablet in his hand—market projections cold and clear. The only sign of time is a red deadline marked on the calendar behind him—silent but urgent.

Seraphina places her prints on the table carefully. She can still feel the tension from the night before: their words had bounced off glass and metal, pressure filling the air like before a storm. The city hums softly outside, and the smell of strong coffee mixes with the clean boardroom air.

Without saying hello, Caius closes his tablet, turns toward her, and speaks. His voice is urgent but controlled—his words sharp, as if he could make the presentation perfect by sheer will.

"We need your story to fit with the firm's current market image. Instinct matters, but data shows our clients like consistency. This," he gestures to her bright cover design, "is confusing. I won't trade clarity for feeling."

She meets his gaze, chin lifted, refusing to back down despite tiredness and pride.

"If clarity is everything, why do your campaigns all look the same? This isn't about comfort. If you want people to remember us, they need to feel something."

He leans forward, hands on the table. "People remember profits, not feelings. Do you want impact or an art show?"

"I want both." She slides mockups across the shiny table—colorful images full of energy and depth. "Show me numbers for emotional campaigns—real connections, not just ROI. Your audience isn't a chart."

His jaw tightens; a pause stretches too long. "Changing the pattern is risky. We're not here to experiment."

"Isn't trust in clients risking something new?" Her voice is soft but firm. "Or do you want the future to look exactly like the past?"

The argument grows sharper, voices rising and overlapping in a familiar and exciting rhythm. Caius offers case studies and risk models, showing the dangers of the unknown. Seraphina answers with stories backed by data and strong visuals, refusing to let numbers kill the spark. She feels frustration building but also a hint of curiosity. At this late hour, surrounded by the city's lights, she sees a man clinging to logic not out of cruelty, but fear—fear of what can't be measured.

As the argument peaks, both glance at the calendar. The deadline's glow pushes them together, stuck as rivals on the same ship.

Caius takes a steady breath, his voice softer now but still firm. "We can't be stuck. If you use our color palette, I'll focus on the story in the campaign's opening—making creativity key in my pitch."

She hesitates, surprised that for once he offers terms instead of orders. Seraphina nods, tapping her touchpad. "Keep the empty space. I need contrast."

He nods. "Done. Move the tagline below the main image—I'll support that in the next meeting."

They work together. Her designs become a little softer; he adjusts bullet points on strategy slides, making room for her story alongside his facts. Hours pass, voices quiet to a steady whisper. Keys click, paper rustles—the quiet teamwork of two strong wills finding a rhythm.

Reviewing the draft, Caius looks up, his face changed—calm but a little gentler.

"You're relentless," he says quietly. "I respect that. Most would have given up or left."

Warmth touches her, unexpected but welcome. "I'm not here just to decorate. Thanks for listening."

In that look, something changes—his guard cracks, and she senses loneliness beneath his discipline. He's not just a machine. There's doubt and hunger there—for connection and meaning—that matches her own strong need to be seen.

She gathers her prints, fighting a smile. He stays by the window, not looking at data but at the city's bright mess of lights. They pause, caught between conflict and understanding, seeing their own defenses in each other.

Something unspoken waits as they leave—no truce, no victory, just silent respect. They walk out carrying pieces of possibility—a fragile curiosity that can't be measured.

In the quiet glass and steel fortress, the morning is unusually still. The city outside rushes under blinking lights, but at the top of the Drake Investment Empire, silence is perfect. Hallways shine with echoes of late-night work. Marcus Langston steps from a private elevator, his polished shoes firm on the marble floor; the soft elevator sound fades into quiet. The CEO's office reacts to his presence; the security panel flickers then goes dark again. The room's silence is so deep that the city's noise feels like a story.

Caius stands against the windows, arms folded calmly. He watches the city stretch far below, his eyes unfocused. The skyline's light traces silver on his suit. Marcus moves with purpose, carrying a confidential folder—a sign of business in a place where feelings aren't expected. He sets the folder on the dark wood desk, breaking up the simple, neat room: one small sculpture, one clock, and now the folder.

"Project update," Marcus says, low and steady. His words are both a question and an order—one he's said many times. Today, the usual rhythm falters. Caius's gaze stays on the window. When he turns, his usual clear armor is weak. His jaw is less tight; his shoulders relax. His eyes slowly follow Marcus.

"The campaign is moving forward," Caius says, his voice less cold. "Hayes's creativity has changed the tone. The presentation feels less cold. The emotional side stands out." He stops, precise but unsure how to balance real feeling with strategy.

"And your thoughts?" Marcus asks, leaning on the table, watching small signs: how Caius's fingers tap lightly on the desk, how strong orders become uncertain replies. Something unseen hangs in the air—the top floor's balance has shifted.

"She's clever. Stubborn. Efficient." A hint of respect appears in his voice. "The work isn't what I'd do alone, but it might be better." Caius doesn't say more. He looks at the folder as if it might explain the change—its papers less important now.

Marcus notices this change carefully. The business world of The Orion Club does not praise weakness; it hunts for it. Caius, once firm and strict, now shows cracks—a mix of wonder and danger. Seraphina brings creativity, warmth, and challenge, but also tears at the control that protects leaders from threats.

"Progress is progress," Marcus says, choosing his words. He watches Caius's reflection in the glass, the city lights behind. He wonders if a softer leader could win or if enemies will attack weakness. Showing kindness comes with risks in a world of secrets and power.

"Do you trust her judgment?" Marcus asks, his voice calm but heavy.

There's a pause—rare honesty fills the space. "I trust her gut, not always her method. She makes me rethink the data." The words mix pride and worry. Caius taps his pen nervously; his usual calm fades.

"You know the board, Caius. Here, openness looks like weakness. Letting someone in—people notice." Marcus's words are soft but serious, warning of dangers ahead. "The Orion Club watches for chances. Trust is rare here."

Caius doesn't react, but silence feels full. Marcus thinks about time and choices. If Caius lets down his guard, will he lose power in a world built on masks? Marcus has known men who tried to balance truth and control—most failed badly.

Will Seraphina make Caius sharper or break his defenses? Marcus imagines paths branching out: one where Caius leads with empathy and gains strong allies, another where enemies smell weakness and attack.

He wants to tell Caius to protect himself more, but he knows the truth: leadership needs both heart and distance. Is that a weakness or a new kind of strength? He cannot tell.

"I hear you," Caius says quietly, but his mind is elsewhere, remembering last night's laughter and arguments, the sharp coffee, and Seraphina's eyes across glass and pixels. He seems stuck between safety in solitude and risk in connection.

Marcus walks to the door, pausing to look at Caius with a look full of unspoken loyalty, worry, and a quiet vow to protect what he can. He leaves, and the office's silence grows deep behind him. Caius stays at the desk, pen in hand, his eyes reflecting the city's glow as if trying to predict the future.

Smoke and Mirrors

The heavy wooden doors closed quietly behind Damien Pierce. The boardroom awaited, lit by a chandelier and filled with unspoken expectations. The leather chairs were old and worn, used by people whose choices had shaped the city. Damien walked steadily across the room, smelling wax, old paper, and cigar smoke that always lingered there. Outside, Manhattan glowed, unaware of the power struggles happening within.

Damien looked at Caius Drake, who sat at the far end of the shiny black table. Caius wore a perfect suit and had a tense jaw. In this room, even a small gesture could be a weapon. Damien's sharp clothes and the scar on his brow felt both useful and unnecessary here.

"This is our latest outside deal, Mr. Drake," Damien said clearly, with no emotion. "Can you explain why you changed plans so late? Some believe the club's good name shouldn't be risked so quickly."

Damien understood risk—the pain of failure and the thrill of winning. But here, where friendships and threats mixed, nothing was simple. Loyalty was just another game.

People whispered quietly. Some nodded to Damien's supporters, showing silent trust. The club was like a living thing, sensing weakness after recent losses. Damien saw an older man's eyes weighing change against tradition.

The room grew quiet as Caius sat up straight and spoke carefully.

"These weeks aren't normal, Mr. Pierce. Taking risks was necessary. Risk drives new ideas. The last-minute change protected things many won't admit," Caius said.

An older man with a rough face leaned forward, unimpressed.

Caius looked at another group at the table's end, his eyes lingering a moment too long. For a second, his eyes showed a question: which way would things go tonight?

Damien felt his heart race but stayed calm—Caius was not unbeatable. The club's story said everyone stood alone, but Damien knew even rulers made deals every night under these lights.

"I suggest we review this emergency decision," Damien said softly but clearly. "Being open protects us more than one man's choice." He raised an eyebrow, a clear challenge. The room grew tense. Some gripped their chairs, fingers tapping nervously.

No one responded. Power changes rarely happen in open fights. First come small signs, then big shifts. Caius remained calm, not reacting. Leaders of the old guard knew when to go with the flow.

Damien leaned back, watching every tense face and secret glance—a kingdom might change here. He felt a brief, sharp control but knew it came at a cost. Deep down, he feared one mistake might mean being cast out. Caius was strong, but his need to hold power was evident to those patient enough to wait.

Chair legs scraped—a sign—and the chairman said, "We will stop for the night." No support or blame, just calm until later. The meeting ended under the slow spin of the chandelier's light.

Caius stood, calm and collected, gathering his papers—the weight of power in his hands. He left slowly, seriousness pressing on him.

Damien waited until the door closed behind Caius, then let out a breath, alert to the murmurs around him. The room filled with quiet, urgent talks. Alliances weren't declared but shown through small moves, looks, and who stayed close to the fire. The air, heavy with old money and cologne, buzzed with secret rivalries and the knowledge that power here was always for sale in silence.

The penthouse office was quiet but tense. A soft light from an LED panel and the city's dark night through glass illuminated the space. Marcus entered quietly, the door shutting softly behind him, cutting them off from the world below—a fortress inside another. Caius stood by the table, one hand on a shiny metal surface, the other holding a glass of whiskey, untouched. The air was tight like a stretched violin string.

He handed Marcus a stack of papers without looking at him. Marcus stepped forward, reading carefully, frowning. Caius gripped the desk tightly; his calm hid his tension.

"Damien's influence is no longer just whispers," Marcus said, his voice low and steady. "Calloway and Suresh listened to him tonight. If we act too quickly, we might split the board. A rash move only wakes the sharks." He leaned on the desk, city lights behind him, far from the secret games happening now.

Caius looked out the window at the dark city lights. The buzz from the meeting lingered with him. Under his controlled surface, old fears stirred. Panic was for the unprepared. He breathed in the faint smell of the city and strong drinks.

"I expected Damien to test me," Caius said slowly. "But I didn't think he'd gain the elders' support so quickly and openly. I underestimated how deep his roots are and how ready they'd be to challenge me if told the right story." He held the glass steady, but his reflection showed doubt and pain. Betrayal was familiar—a childhood filled with broken promises and trust used as a bargain.

He imagined what would happen if he lost control now. The board would turn against him, secret talks becoming weapons. This was normal for survival at this level, but tonight suggested worse tricks might happen soon.

"Then we use old tactics," Marcus said calmly. "Sometimes a slow, quiet plan works best. Olivia is near the middle—she's careful and loyal to order, not just power. Bring Barnes into the plan quietly. Show her what you've built and what's coming. I'll spread reminders to less involved members about the successes and risks of sudden change. Make them doubt Damien before they support him. Loyalty here isn't about feelings; it's about fear, ambition, and keeping what they have. Use that. I'll handle the details. You control the story."

Caius turned from the city, his hand gripping a chair. For a moment, his mask slipped; his jaw moved as he spoke softly, almost begging. "I can't seem weak. If they see that, I'm finished. Marcus—" His voice cracked. "I don't know who's loyal anymore. I see cracks everywhere. What if this gets out of control?"

Marcus came closer and placed a steady hand on Caius's shoulder, a rare gesture full of years of loyalty. "A smart attack turns whispers into shields, not swords. Let allies share stories—half-truths they think they found themselves. You don't need every vote, just enough confusion to stop Damien. Loyalty here is about self-interest, not love. Use that. I'll manage the moves. You lead."

They worked through the papers, listing names, notes, weaknesses—each a tool or risk for their secret war. Marcus worked on the outer members while Caius planned to talk to Olivia. Their plans spread into the night.

When Caius finally looked up, his eyes were hard. Marcus met his gaze, understanding each other without words. The city's fake morning light glowed behind them. Caius stared out again, his plan coming together. Doubt was still there but hidden by firm resolve. Both men knew how thin the line was between ruling and falling.

Seraphina sat cross-legged on a worn Persian rug, the red pattern faded, gold threads sticking out. She held a heavy mug, swirling it gently—it was hot with a sharp coffee flavor and citrus. The lounge was quiet in the early afternoon light, sunlight spilling through big windows. Seraphina watched the activity outside, her eyes dark with worry.

Caius walked across the marble lobby, his figure sharp in the metal light. His steps were quick and soft, his suit clean and perfect. He spoke quietly with security staff, standing stiff as if expecting danger. The guards nodded in agreement, their badges shining in the LED light. Each meeting was short and coded, a warning unspoken. Seraphina pursed her lips, sensing the sudden tension in the calm lobby.

Something felt wrong. Staff near the lounge's entrance checked security cameras more often than usual; the cameras hummed softly under the music playing. Keycard readers blinked repeatedly from frequent use. Seraphina's eyes sharpened; she saw signs of caution—a careful dance meant to protect either an important person or secrets close to being revealed. Her heart sped up. A junior executive, red-faced and messy, hurried by and stopped when Olivia Barnes spoke quietly to him through a door crack:

"We need more privacy for all secret files. Any leaks—"

The young man nodded, tense. They disappeared around the corner, their shoes soft on the carpet. Seraphina felt the back of her neck prickle—something hidden was changing, shifting the power around them.

She stood up, the rug curling under her foot, and moved to a snack counter near the shadowed lounge. Jasper was there, bent over a bowl of candied nuts, his fingers sticky.

"Hey, Jasp. Heard anything strange today?" she whispered, wanting secrets, not comfort.

Jasper shrugged, smirking a bit. "Nothing except Olivia on the warpath." He stuffed some nuts in his pocket and looked at her sideways. "Why? Am I supposed to have all the answers now?"

"That'd be easier," Seraphina muttered. As Jasper turned back to the coffee machine, a memory struck her—last night, before sleep, she'd heard voices near the stairwell: members talking about a coming reckoning, new groups forming—like storms gathering overhead. She remembered the fear in those whispers. Jasper didn't notice as he walked away, but the memory left her uneasy, like brushing against a sharp edge of the future.

The feeling of uncertainty grew. Seraphina returned to her mug, the warmth barely comforting. She watched Caius stop two analysts, his smile polite but careful, never meeting her eyes even as she moved closer.

"Caius," she said, her voice full of worry.

He paused, barely smiling, eyes flicking past her. "Sorry—back-to-back meetings today," he said smoothly but distantly.

She looked at him, searching for a sign he would open up. Her hand twitched. "Is everything okay after last night's meeting?"

His mouth tightened before softening. "We'll talk later. I have it under control."

He walked away before she could ask more, his posture closed, jaw stiff. Seraphina was left with his scent and a cold feeling of being shut out—familiar and frustrating. She knew she was being kept away from the center of the storm, though the storm surrounded her now.

The city glowed in the cold winter light outside the big windows. Seraphina faced her own reflection, jaw tight, tracing her tattoo with her thumb. She promised herself: no more waiting for answers, no more letting problems go unseen. She would watch for cracks in voices, soft thuds of secret files, tiny signs of power moving. To survive here—and to help Caius stay steady—she had to understand the language of hidden motives.

She moved to a corner chair and opened her sketchbook. Her pen raced over rough paper, writing names, half-heard phrases—reckoning, alliances, Olivia's warning, Jasper's evasions. Outside the glass, Caius disappeared into a secure elevator, a figure moving away in a world full of light and danger. Seraphina looked after him, alert to the storms gathering just beneath the surface.

Fractures

Afternoon light breaks through the glass walls, casting amber shapes across Caius's office. The city spreads out below, busy and bright. The quiet of the marble room is broken by the sound of Evelyn's heels clicking sharply. She walks in without pausing, the door closing smoothly behind her. Her eyes pass over Caius's stiff nod, ignoring formalities. She moves forward, her dark hair glowing in the sunlight, every step full of purpose. Her voice is firm and tense.

"You thought I wouldn't notice? Tell me, Caius. Did you think I'd just accept you ruining the foundation for your new project? Or is that another 'family priority' I'm supposed to ignore?"

Sunlight shines on the chrome details of the room, reflecting off metal sculptures that stand like silent guards. Caius rises from his chair, careful and tense. His face remains polite but strained. He looks out at the city for a moment, as if it protects him, then he turns and speaks flatly.

"This isn't the right time, Evelyn. The decision had to be made quickly. The foundation isn't my only concern."

She sneers sharply. Her fists clench, nails digging into her palms, marking the pain of being shut out. "Urgent—funny how your urgent needs always come first. Just like Dad's urgent meetings. Remember those? He'd go to 'important dinners,' and we'd eat cold leftovers alone. Did you feel better knowing you picked up both his job and his habits?"

His voice tightens, panic showing. "That's not fair. Things aren't that simple—"

She cuts him off coldly, "No, they never were with you. Not once. Especially after Dad started grooming you to be his shadow." She remembers being thirteen in their childhood library, waiting for some sign of care while their father pulled Caius into secret lessons about legacy and control. Streetlight came through the old glass, casting lines over chessboards and books, teaching them that love meant achievement and silence meant loyalty.

The words hang between them, sharp and tense.

"You keep making excuses, Caius, as if you don't see it—how you erase anything that doesn't fit your perfect story. Did you ever think about what I wanted? Or was it always about saving your reputation and maintaining the 'Drake image'?"

His jaw tightens, an old habit. He walks to the windows slowly, each step deliberate, as their father taught—standing still was giving in. The office hums with distant city noise, but inside, time feels frozen: just the marble floor, the bright sun, and the memory and blame between them.

His voice is tense. "You think I wanted this? You think I don't…" He sees his reflection in the glass, showing two scars—one visible above his eyebrow, one deeper and hidden. He turns, his voice breaking. "I'm so tired, Evelyn. Tired of fighting. Of carrying his failures like my own. I did what I had to—and I paid for it every time."

Her anger softens, revealing old pain. Tears come and go in her eyes. She remembers nights listening for any sign of authority, hoping for a word or a touch that meant sacrifice wasn't abandonment. She recalls cold roast chicken, the silence after slammed doors, and being told she was "a Drake, with all that means." That meant learning to hide softness behind calculation and to mistrust her own voice when power was near.

"Maybe you paid," she says, her voice rough. "But you never looked back to see who else was left behind."

She shakes her head and turns sharply, cold marble under her shoes. Her feet echo down the hall, a steady sound of loss and unfinished business. The glass breaks her shape as she leaves, leaving only quiet and the words they couldn't say.

Caius sinks into his chair, shoulders slumping. The last light falls on the metal arcs and dark surfaces by the window. The door is closed, but Evelyn's pain lingers in the air. He covers his face with his hands, his posture breaking the strong image the office demands.

Alone, the city's heartbeat feels empty through the glass. Metal sculptures cast sharp shadows on his desk—symbols of order and chaos balanced together. Caius sits still as memories swirl around him, heavy and unfinished in the cooling twilight.

The lounge is almost empty, its clean lines softened by warm LED lights over black leather chairs. Glass walls hide the night, dulling the city's busy sounds to a faint hum. Seraphina sits at a small teak table near a short plant, her sleeves rolled up as a stylus moves quickly over her tablet. The faint tapping is the only sound. Caius appears in the doorway—his shoulders tense, movements slow, light catching a small scar above his brow and dark circles under his eyes. His suit is neat but a bit rumpled, as if he forgot how to wear it.

He pauses at the door, his eyes moving from a bronze sculpture behind Seraphina to her scattered pencils and graphite sketches. A quiet tension fills the space as he walks to her table.

He sits across from her, hands flat on the table, fingers shaking slightly. The space between them feels heavy, full of waiting.

"You're working late," Caius says, his voice softer than it should be.

Seraphina doesn't look up right away. "Deadlines don't wait just because it gets quiet at night."

His eyes follow her stylus. The words he wants to say press at his throat—sharp, unfinished, urgent. He breathes slowly, the scent of coffee and faint cologne nearby.

"I fought with Evelyn," he says after a moment, his voice cracking. "She said I gave up everything for power. That I erased what the family stood for." He laughs hollowly. "She's not wrong."

He hesitates, watching the light around her hair. "Every choice I make feels like dealing with ghosts—my father's expectations, the club's secrets." Saying "secrets" is hard, like letting something dangerous loose. "I have to pretend I know what I'm doing, that I'm not affected. But the truth is—" He stops, his jaw tight as he swallows the rest.

Seraphina puts the stylus down and folds her arms on the table, relaxed and calm. She doesn't try to fill the silence; she lets it stretch, a safe space, not a threat.

"No one is really untouched behind all that armor," she says quietly. "Your sister sounded hurt. But you did too."

His lips press together. His mind is loud, sorting through hidden memories—nights pacing in empty hallways, the taste of whiskey left to go bad on his tongue, voices from childhood fading down marble halls. The rules their father gave: never trust, never falter, always hide feelings. Now, with Seraphina looking at him clearly, he feels the mask he wears start to come undone.

The silence stays, a space neither wants to leave.

"I never wanted this," he says. "Not the empire, not the high place. It was always the cost—my choices were never really mine, not after..." His voice trails off as if the past cuts off the sentence.

"Must be lonely," Seraphina says kindly.

He blinks, not used to the feeling—envy sharp inside. He looks at her hands, touched with graphite. "You don't owe anyone. You make things. You get to decide what's yours." His voice reveals a quiet longing.

Seraphina's face softens. She moves one hand from her sketchbook and lays it on the table, palm up, reaching halfway. The gesture is shy, as if standing at the edge of a cliff, but it's an offer.

Their fingers don't touch, but a connection hums—a quiet closeness against all the things left unsaid.

"I don't always feel so free," she whispers. "But I try to be honest. With myself, with others. Maybe that's the only kind of freedom there is."

He looks at her hand. The urge to reach out surprises him—after a lifetime of locking his feelings away. Instead, his thumb moves silently across the table.

Outside the lounge, city lights flicker—car headlights making rivers of light between tall buildings made for giants and shadows. Inside, the last staff leave, their footsteps and soft laughs fading down the hall.

Neither moves. The air is full of a fragile newness, as delicate as glass and as real as hope.

Their eyes meet, and beneath the cold corporate mask, something is shared. For a moment, their burdens split in two, warmed by each other's softness. No words. Just a quiet that speaks of pain, longing, and the first crack in the walls around them.

One by one, lights go out along the hallway behind them. Caius and Seraphina stay in the quiet, two figures lit by soft light, caught between sharing and shutting down, until finally they part—changed, if only by what they showed and what they left unsaid.

Seraphina settles into her old leather chair, worn smooth by years spent working late. Her dark apartment is dim, lit only by city lights through thin curtains, casting shifting patterns on her paint-stained desk. She looks out the window, lost in the headlights winding between rooftops below. Caius's low, shaky voice replays in her mind—each word sharp and cold. She watches for movement outside, but the world feels frozen, like a painting before its last stroke.

"Why do I even think about this?" she whispers. Trust is something she has learned to avoid, not to grow. The city sometimes feels like a maze haunted by ghosts—her footsteps echoing at doors she can't open. Her cat, Monarch, flicks its tail on the windowsill, watching as if it expects an answer.

She breathes out slowly, trying to calm the noise inside her. "You'd think I'd know better. Power only leaves marks." Her voice shakes but remains brave. The silence answers with the faint noise of an old heater, distant sirens, and the beat of her worries.

She's cut ties with people who wore armor instead of warmth too many times. Years working two jobs after losing her father's money, years fighting to pay rent and care for her mother, years making art in rare free moments—this struggle made her strong but careful. She once believed in a promise of safety, only to find herself lost, the story ending before she named it. The lesson came hard: independence is the safest shield, the only one she can trust. Yet now there's a new feeling, a longing in her chest shaped by Caius's grief. He isn't safe, she knows that—and even less so now that she's seen his honest edges.

Her hand moves before she thinks. She pulls out her worn tablet and starts to sketch, the stylus shaking with nervous energy. On the screen, she draws two forms in shades of gray: one sharp and controlled with straight lines; the other loose and flowing, edges soft as if moved by wind. She presses harder, trying to blend them. The stiff lines resist but soften as the wild tendrils reach out, finding a way to fit. Each stroke is hope fighting fear, growth battling the urge to protect herself.

Her thoughts rush in: Is there kindness in a world ruled by power? She recalls her mother's hand on her shoulder in hard times—a love when nothing else was there. She thinks of a gallery owner who laughed when she refused to change her art for money, and the fierce pride of staying true. She remembers how easy it is to close off after every loss, to become smaller and harder. But tonight she resists; the memory of Caius's pain is a small fire she won't let go.

Her hand hesitates over the twisted shapes. Monarch jumps into her lap, kneading her jeans and purring steadily. The purr grounds her; warmth flows into her legs, holding her in the moment. She sets the tablet down and strokes Monarch's striped back. The city beyond is a swirl of color and light, proving that even chaos makes patterns if you watch long enough.

She breathes in the mix of paint, cool air, and fur, letting it settle deep. Then, barely louder than a secret, she says, "No more running. Not from myself. Not from him." Her words fade into the quiet, trembling but firm.

For a while, Seraphina listens to the city's soft noises—the pipes ticking, cars far below, laughter trickling up from cracked sidewalks. Her courage feels fragile, still forming, much like the sketch glowing on her tablet. But she holds it carefully, like a seed. She leans back,

Monarch purring against her, and lets her eyes soften over the rough, flowing lines—together at last. In the silence, she gathers her strength, ready or not, for whatever the dark brings next.

Crossing Boundaries

The sound of the meeting room still lingers, a mix of raised voices bouncing off the clean glass and dark wood. Caius stands alone, quiet and still after the others have left. The setting sun shines on the shiny table, casting bright lines across his polished shoes. Even though the arguments have ended, the room feels tense—a feeling created by hope and pressure.

Seraphina quickly gathers her notebook and tablet. Her fingers move quickly, hiding the slight shake in her hands. She avoids looking at anyone and stares at her worn notepad, pressing her thumb on the edge—a habit to stop feeling watched. Her breath smells faintly of aftershave and fresh air, and the cold room feels sharp as she walks away.

Caius's quiet but firm voice breaks the silence. He signals for Seraphina to come with him. After a quick glance at the last person leaving, he leads her to a quiet corner near the executive offices. Large metal and bronze sculptures stand tall like guards, casting patterns on the bright walls. Here, everything seems smaller—only the distant sounds of the city and the fading sun through the glass connect them to the world below.

He faces the window, standing straight and tense. For a moment, he says nothing, staring at the metal art as if trying to understand it. Then he relaxes a bit; his voice, usually sharp and commanding, becomes softer and more personal.

"The pressure never goes away," he says. "People expect more and more each day. I have to always seem sure, never doubting."

Seraphina crosses her arms—not to defend herself, but to hold herself steady, as if she might disappear behind the statues. The sun makes a golden line along her jaw. Her clear, restless eyes watch him. Around them, time seems to stop: no clocks ticking, no assistants talking—just the city's distant hum.

High above the river, Caius shares what others don't see. Each word is carefully chosen, unlike his usual instinct. His authority feels like borrowed armor; beneath it, his skin tightens with memories—a rival's betrayal, cold family dinners, and a scar that haunts him. The empire he runs is like a delicate web made of glass, metal, and hidden stories.

Seraphina's voice is softer than expected, less sure than at work, more like a quiet before a landslide. "Your world doesn't need people like me. When I see these glass and steel walls, I wonder if I'm just fading away. Every time I speak at meetings, I worry it takes a piece of me. I don't know how to fit here without losing myself."

Her honesty changes the room—it feels smaller, closer, not physically but emotionally. Her words crack the confidence she shows the world, revealing the real feelings underneath.

Caius looks down at the bronze sculptures, his voice low. "Control is all I trust. But it's lonely. I've made myself into a weapon sharp enough to hurt even the ones I care about." His face reflects in the window, half shadow, half light. "You challenge that. I don't know if I want to push you away or keep you close, because both are hard."

A heavy silence grows between them. In that quiet, doubt lives—alive and tense. The world around them doesn't change—this strong fortress is built to keep surprises out—but inside it, they feel unsure, as if the ground might slip away.

Seraphina straightens. She drops her arms and softens her face, letting him see her vulnerability. She nods slightly, a start of something unspoken but real. Then, her shadow stretching beside his, she turns away, leaving him with the fading light, the statues, and the city view he can't fully control—not now, not with her in his life.

###

Warm light fills Seraphina's café, broken by green ivy climbing the windows. The city feels far away, almost like a dream she can choose to look at or ignore. She walks inside, welcomed by soft golden light and the smell of cinnamon and coffee. She sinks into a comfy armchair, the tiredness of the day catching up with her. The cushions remember her shape, offering comfort no fancy office can provide. Her bag falls from her shoulder to the floor. She looks at her hands—the pencil smudge under her nail, the dark ink tattoo on her wrist, her fingers clenching and unclenching as she tries to find the courage to open up.

Jasper stands behind the counter, relaxed and chatting with a regular. He smiles at her, friendly and easygoing. Here, with walls colored warm brown, he feels like part of the furniture—a patchwork friend sitting next to her.

He sets two hot mugs on the table, the coffee's rich smell rising, and pushes a flaky pastry toward her. Soft music plays: a sad guitar tune that rises and falls slowly like waves. Seraphina feels it calm her heart; her body remembers simpler, softer rhythms far from the sharp edges of Drake Investments.

"So," Jasper says, sitting across from her, one leg tucked under him. "You look like you fought with a room full of vampires—how bad was it?"

Seraphina looks past him, words slow to come. "They speak in puzzles. Every answer has layers, and I don't know if I should figure them out or just pretend to be impressed."

"On a scale of one to ten for scary?"

"Try thirteen. And Caius—" she stops, the name strange and personal, too close for work talk, too far for secrets.

Jasper leans forward. "Let me guess. He gave you the CEO look like he was measuring your worth?"

A small smile appears. "He wasn't bad. He actually spoke about pressure, about expectations. Like he wanted me to see the person behind the mask for once." Her eyes search, unsure, as she tells her story.

"That messed with my head. For two minutes, I almost forgot he's just a human behind spreadsheets and stress."

"That's progress. Probably listed right after 'quarterly growth' in the business manual."

She laughs softly, but her voice still carries tiredness. "I don't belong there, Jasp. It's all marble and glass, and me with my old bag, trying to remember when to ask questions or stay quiet. I feel like I'm falling into something I can't escape."

He breaks the pastry and offers half. "Eat. You'll need energy for round two."

"What if that place takes away the things I like about myself? What if I stop fighting and one day I wake up no longer stubborn?"

"You're too stubborn to let that happen. The day Seraphina Hayes gets crushed by suits with 'Legacy' in their email is the day I eat a kale salad by choice."

She laughs fully now, the sound loosening the tightness in her chest.

They sit in quiet. Around them, the café hides lone artists and groups of friends. Here, being open costs nothing but a cup of coffee and trust.

Seraphina's mind is still heavy with memories. The harsh laughs in the elevator, Olivia's judging look, her own reflection in the glass—a ghost outside. She wears fear like armor, mixed with proud defiance. Every day at Drake is a deal: how much of herself to keep, how much to give up to survive. What if they slowly smooth away the rough edges she needs?

Jasper holds the moment gently. "You don't have to split in two. You just need a plan—and some escape routes when they start talking like financial experts. Remember last fall, when you handled that art project and three jobs? You planned every minute and still made time for bad karaoke."

"I forgot about that," she says quietly. "Maybe I just need a plan again."

"Exactly. Art first. Everything else fits around it or not at all. I'll help you make a schedule and remind you to eat. Deal?"

"Deal." Hope feels bold in her mouth, sudden and real. "No matter how hard this gets, I won't let them take away the parts of me that matter."

He lifts his coffee like a toast. "I won't let them either. You keep fighting, and I'll keep feeding you pastries and pep talks about dealing with billionaires."

She smiles, warmed by the pastry and promise. Between the soft chair and Jasper's steady presence, the city's harsh cold loses its grip—at least for tonight.

###

In the grand Drake Investments lobby, Olivia Barnes stands apart from the busy crowd of executives and investors. Her posture is perfect, and her eyes are sharp. The marble floor reflects the soft light from the modern chandeliers—designed to feel like daylight but failing to warm the cold mood underneath. People talk quietly and laugh forcedly. Every move is careful, as if they're preparing for a fight no one can see.

Near the elevators, Caius stands clearly next to Seraphina Hayes. Olivia watches her closely; Seraphina still seems new here, no matter her neat jacket or steady walk. They stand close, sharing a quiet moment while others move in careful circles. Olivia notices how Caius tilts his head and how Seraphina hesitates—small signs that their talk matters. It could change things if you know how to read the hidden currents of the city.

The culture here is a mix of magic and suspicion—a world built on secrets and glass walls. Loyalty is rare and valuable, traded in secret looks and whispers, held together not by trust but by fear. Outsiders, no matter how polished, must pass an invisible test watched by security and the firm's true guardians. It is a place where power is dangerous, old money and ambition mixed in strong steel, and newcomers are never trusted right away. Every alliance is unspoken, judged, and can become a weapon.

Olivia moves through the busy room, brushing against cool marble pillars, her fingers wrapped around a nearly empty crystal glass. She spots Michael Cort, her oldest friend there. Her voice is quiet, meant only for him.

"Have you noticed how fast Seraphina is blending with the partners?" Olivia's smile is thin and polite.

Michael nods slightly, not looking over. "Caius values efficiency. She's definitely... flexible."

"Flexible," Olivia repeats. She pauses as voices hum nearby. "Or maybe something less clear. Moving up fast usually has a price. We can't let feelings get in the way at this level."

He studies her face but sees nothing clear. "You think she's a risk?"

"I think," Olivia says softly, "being careful is a tradition for a reason. Especially now. We can't afford mistakes—no matter how charming the person." Her words are polite but sharp, a warning.

He considers this, then says, "Noted."

She watches him leave toward the private elevator, his steps quiet on the shiny floor. For a moment, Olivia thinks about how these walls keep secrets and how even now, the building seems to listen.

She slips behind a pillar into shadow. The lobby's noise fades. She pulls out her tablet and swipes quickly. Her reflection flashes as lines of code and personnel files fill the screen. She checks Seraphina's records—work history, connections, strange gaps that raise questions.

Her notes are clear: "Fast rise. Unusual access. Watch for problems. Check outside contacts."

Her chest tightens—a familiar pain—but she holds steady. Old mistakes haunt her here, memories no audit can erase. Control, always control—losing it now could break everything. Trust is just a story to keep order. She can't let feelings or risks slip through, for anyone, not even herself.

Golden light pools at her feet as footsteps echo. Across the room, Seraphina stands near the edge, unaware of Olivia watching. Others see her too, judging if she will be a shining star or a disaster. Olivia's gaze stays sharp and cold like a hunter.

Tonight, curiosity becomes resolve. Tomorrow, Olivia plans to turn doubt into proof. For now, she waits in the dark, watching Seraphina's next move, while the city's steady pulse sounds beneath the walls of glass and steel.

Storm Approaches

The shiny marble floor reflects the fluorescent lights above. It shows quick reflections of workers waiting by the elevators and the glass ceiling grid overhead. Between the elevators and the executive offices, quiet conversations move through the halls, as if the building itself is nervous, passing worries from one floor to another. A new fear is growing—that the company's strength might just be an illusion, ready to fall apart with one failure.

People whisper words like "sabotage," "data breach," and "offshore losses." Some tap on their tablets, searching for news or deleting digital traces that pass through servers hidden behind fancy walls. The sound of shoes on marble is too fast, too urgent for such a serious place, signaling that orders are coming. People avoid looking at closed glass doors, not wanting to meet hard stares. On the 80th floor, trust disappears like morning condensation.

Caius Drake steps into his office, glass walls providing a clear view of New York's skyline—sharp but distant. The room feels cold. Marcus stands by the desk, holding a manila folder. Caius takes it and unfolds the papers, illuminated by a soft LED screen. The report is full of timestamps, IP addresses, and transfers that shouldn't exist—accounts emptied without mistakes. Each has a pattern.

Sabotage. The word stands out in the file.

Caius hardly reacts. A small muscle twitches above his scar. He reads more slowly now, steadying his mind. He feels the weight of New York under his feet—the buildings, the trading floors, the rivals watching closely. He types a message, calling for a board meeting. His jaw tightens; nothing shows the tremor inside.

The boardroom is silent and tense, the air cold and clean. Olivia sits near him, her scar visible in the harsh light. Others wear black suits and silver cuffs, their faces tired from worry. They look at Caius as he speaks.

"There's been unauthorized access to our systems. It was someone inside, on purpose. We have a breach, maybe a mole."

Tension fills the room, heavy and quiet. Partners shift in their seats. Olivia looks between Caius and Marcus, her voice sharp.

"How bad?"

"Seven accounts hit. Illegal transfers were made at times to avoid notice," Marcus says clearly.

Murmurs break out like static noise.

"We're doubling internal checks. No leaks, no outside interviews. Any problem, no matter how small, comes to me," Caius says firmly.

No one argues. The cost of being exposed here is too high.

Outside, Seraphina's steps slow by the frosted glass doors. She holds her design papers, their colored edges visible through her shaking fingers. The sounds inside are muted—footsteps, papers rustling, names of accounts like foreign words. Through the frosted glass, she hears Olivia's low, urgent question.

"Are we sure it's not someone in Compliance? Or..."

Marcus answers, cautious and suspicious, "Nothing is certain. We must consider all possibilities."

Seraphina feels the cold from the marble floor seep into her bones. The thought that suspicion may follow her in looks and greetings cracks her certainty.

The Drake Investment Empire was built on secrets—power kept quiet, deals made in private talks, loyalty bought. This is a world where sabotage is like war, a threat that feels personal. A small rumor of "a mole" can turn coworkers into enemies and start fights disguised as duty. The board's tough competition is a maze of shifting loyalties, each executive holding onto their power, afraid to be accused or lose status. Now, in this fog of distrust, the company's image of strength grows thin. Even Caius can't control the chaos when trust is broken and fake.

As Marcus takes his orders and partners gather their papers, sharing silent nods filled with old grudges and hopes, the board's confidence unravels. Caius watches them with cold gray eyes shaped by years at the top. Showing weakness would invite attackers; showing fear is not an option. He feels an old pain—the loneliness of being the leader. Every move costs him more trust and isolates him further.

The meeting ends quietly. Caius's last words are clear: "No mistakes. I want reports every hour. You are dismissed."

As the heavy doors open, Seraphina slips back into the maze of halls, her heartbeat quickening with the threat that rumors are now the strongest weapons—ones her art or cleverness can't protect her from. The door closing seals the tension, promising consequences that won't stay hidden.

Amber light passes through thick curtains in the Orion Club's private lounge, illuminating smoke from cigars and the sharp edges of the whiskey glass in Damien Pierce's hand. He sits with two old club members, their shapes more rumor than reality in the dark corner. Their red velvet booth keeps secrets; between polished wood and shiny cufflinks, they talk in quiet, careful voices.

Damien leans in, his voice smooth, almost like a secret. "Unheard of," he says, swirling his drink. "Drake's firm—system failures, sabotage, money disappearing. You'd think the Orion would expect more from its protectors." His smile is thin and sharp—meant to hurt but seem harmless. The first man, an old banker with deep lines, raises an eyebrow, interested. "You think this will stay contained?" he asks quietly. The other, a powerful financier, just exhales smoke—a silent, serious answer.

Damien lets silence grow. At the Orion, what you don't say matters more than what you do. Suspicion feels built into the old woodwork. Eyes flick to the open floor and closed doors beyond. "We trust the leaders to protect what's important," Damien says finally, looking at a large oil portrait of a long-dead founder. "But sometimes empires break from the inside, not the outside."

A quiet agreement forms—weak, uncertain, tied together by whispered doubts. Here, friendships are made in the space between raised glasses and avoided eyes. Today, doubt is growing with every secret word.

Damien's plan moves forward with skill as the day goes on. In quiet halls smelling of old books and polish, he moves between rooms, always calm. His phone glows blue in his hand—a tool for power. He calls, his voice low as he spreads doubt, placing it like smoke among tall buildings. "Security problems trace back to leaders, my friend," he whispers to an ally. "Maybe it's time for a steadier leader—or at least backup plans." Messages fly, rumors spread. The powerful listen closely for signs of weakness.

Each conversation feeds fading loyalties. Calls end with unclear replies: "We'll see what happens." Damien's heart beats fast with hope—he feels he is close to winning, tasting it in the whiskey and secret shifts of loyalty in this old club.

Behind a heavy door with the club's crest, Caius listens as Marcus gives his report calmly. The room is quiet but electric—walls lined with books, the light smell of cigar hiding under wood and cedar. Marcus's words are short, low enough to not be heard by the curtains. "Damien is stirring trouble, Caius. I hear doubts from those we thought loyal—he's saying your leadership is a risk. Calls, casual meetings, secret questions about who comes next."

Caius's jaw tightens, his reflection broken in the glass he holds. Patterns form in his mind: every member could be a mercenary, torn between fear and ambition each day. The Orion always plays a double game; loyalty is money, trust a gift, betrayal the rule. He imagines how quickly everything might fall apart. One more mistake, another breach, and the elders might side with Damien—someone they trust to stay clear of scandal.

The tension coils in Caius's chest. Should he confront Damien openly, or quietly build his own network to choke out rumors? Which friends has he missed—who is ready to stab him? So much depends on tonight and what happens next. He plans a silent counterattack—flexible, hidden—but winning over Damien will take more than tactics; it needs charm, clear thinking, and a readiness to go deeper if needed. He worries that in protecting everything, he might lose the club's quiet trust, the bond that connects power to his name.

Cocktail hour brings the conflict into open view. Decanters glow gold under the ballroom lights. Damien stands by the polished bar, relaxed but sharp. "One wonders," he says, looking at Caius but speaking to everyone, "how sure can we be that our interests are safe with so many problems at the Empire?" Laughter stops. Eyes turn sharply. The air feels tense.

A pause. Caius meets the gaze, standing tall, his words steady like armor. "The Orion's interests are my main concern. Security issues will be fixed by nightfall on my watch."

Damien's smile is cold, like melting ice in Scotch, and he turns away. The crowd murmurs, the night's balance shifting under the chandeliers. Their eyes meet once more—a rivalry marked by hunger and silent promises of battles ahead.

Seraphina's apartment grows quiet as the city slows outside the window. Moonlight shines softly through thin curtains, casting a cool light. The worn Persian rug under her feet is old but strong—a reminder of simpler times. The old cat purrs at her knee, eyes half-closed, while her phone's blue screen lights her face. One message shines at the top—sharp, secret, no name: "They say you're compromised. That you don't belong to us anymore. Watch out."

She freezes, her breath shallow. The words turn her peaceful home into a fragile cage. Rugs, pots, paintings—all pieces of herself shake under suspicion. The room's warmth shrinks; her fingers grip the phone tightly. She always knew the risks—creativity and independence overshadowed by Caius's powerful empire. But suspicion hurts deeper than she expected. Every noise—the distant traffic, the cat's soft purr—feels like the city is listening for her next move.

Under her desk lamp's glow, she reads the message again. Her mind flits through snippets of workplace talk, looks exchanged, forced smiles in bright halls. She loves the city's fast pace, but its secrets eat away at her: in Caius's world, every kindness is a trade, every friend a deal. To belong means giving up something important. The bitter taste of that truth lingers with her tonight.

She stands, feeling the cold floor through her feet, and moves to her old desk. Paintbrushes and tangled cords spill over each other, signs of order and mess. The phone's glass feels hard in her hand, her thumb hovering over Jasper's name. She imagines his dry jokes—the comfort of his voice after years. He'd want to help. But she tastes the risk: one rumor could turn into more suspicion, Jasper's trust used against them both. In this world, weakness is a crack power rushes to fill.

She thinks about calling anyway. Maybe she could be brave enough to tell him what she hides—that loyalty is complicated, that fear mixes with ambition and friendship. Before Caius, vulnerability was a luxury—quiet talks late at night, soft mornings. Here, among glass towers and whispered betrayals, showing yourself is a danger just beneath the skin. She recalls when a team turned on her, how silent rooms felt full of judgment, how giving up tasted—like metal and melting ice.

Suddenly, her thumb moves away from Jasper's name. She sets the phone face down on a sketch of a bird in flight. Shadows move across the picture. There is strength in this choice, though her shoulders ache from the cost. Facing doubts alone—without leaning on others—is another kind of faith in who she is. Vulnerability might be the one rebellion left in a world of steel and schemes.

Later, she walks across the city's steel streets, the cold air sharp on her face as she leaves her safe home. At night, the Drake Investment Empire's headquarters rise like a cold glass tower; the building's walls reflect nothing back, hiding the city's chaos but making the inside feel empty. Security lets her in; her steps sound on marble as she moves toward the top floor, nerves fluttering.

Caius's office is a glass box of bright light and dark night, windows showing the skyline. The LED light makes everything clear, leaving no room for confusion or comfort. He stands by his desk, still and watchful. Papers and screens scatter reflections on shiny metal.

She doesn't hesitate. Seraphina straightens up, her senses sharp from tiredness and adrenaline.

"I'm not leaving, no matter what they say. I'm committed to this project—for you, for myself—and no one can shake that with rumors." Her voice is clear and steady. "But it's hard to stand in the middle of all this. If you think I'm a problem—say it. I won't let rumors ruin me or push me out for someone else's mistakes."

Caius's gaze softens, something uncertain showing behind his cold eyes. His body relaxes; his mouth eases. For a moment, he looks almost soft.

"You're not a problem. They're just scared. I trust you. That matters." His words fill the space between them—they are rare and heavy, as if neither truly believed in trust until now.

A strange connection forms—two people lost in a storm of plans, finding brief safety in honesty.

He says no more. She meets his eyes, sharing their tired but determined feelings. For a moment, they don't speak; no masks, no acting, just the truth of surviving.

When Seraphina leaves the office, the quiet space feels like a second skin, her heart thumping. But she stands taller, each step bracing against the cold. Behind the glass wall, Caius watches her go, hope flickering quietly as the city's darkness surrounds them both.

Breaking Point

Night covers the city like a dark blanket, pressing against the glass walls of Caius Drake's office. Rain falls on the windows, breaking the city lights into many small reflections. The lights outside are cold and harsh, always on, never resting. Inside, the office feels stuffy—a place of control and careful planning, where mistakes are stopped before they cause damage. Under the desk, Caius holds a secret report, full of data and warnings. The company's future depends on it. He stands with his back to the city, lit by a bright panel that resembles daylight. For a moment, the office feels like an empire ready to fall.

"We do this now," he says, his voice sharp and firm. "We cut twice as much. We freeze all non-essential departments. We can't be careless. Someone broke our security, and half the board wants to blame others."

"You want to lock everyone up and call it progress?" Seraphina's voice breaks the silence. She stands by the window, her hair messy as if she just came in from the rain. "How can the creative team trust you if you treat us like things—replaceable and quiet? You'll kill every bit of creativity here. Is that really what you want?"

Caius tightens his grip on the folder. The room feels smaller, made of glass and polished wood, as if even the metal sculptures are listening to see who will give in first. He walks around the desk, his eyes cold and firm. "This is about keeping the firm alive, Seraphina. Do you think your designers will have jobs if we lose everything? Control is what keeps chaos away." His words are harsh. "You think morale can balance the books or fix security. You don't know what's at risk—at all."

"Oh, I know what's at risk," Seraphina says, stepping closer, her fingers shaking. "Your legacy. Your empire. But you'd destroy the spirit of every person here just to pass another audit. You talk about chaos, but what about the chaos you bring by shutting down the people who built this company? What do you really care about, besides your reflection in all this glass?"

Inside Caius, a storm rages—a silent battle. Years of pressure weigh down on him. He remembers his father's cold voice, saying failure was shame; the Drakes were meant to win or lose everything. He felt this like a heavy chain. When he was thirteen, he first faced betrayal—his sister turned away, a friend sold secrets for revenge. Something inside him closed then. He vowed it would never happen again. Walls and fear are all he knows—walls and the thought that someone waits for him to fail.

"This isn't easy for me," he shouts, his voice rough from the strain he hides. "You think I wanted this?" He slams the report on the desk. "If I lose control, everything my family built will break. One mistake, and it's gone. I won't let that happen."

Seraphina flinches, her face flushed. Her hands shake as she holds the desk. The city's faint noise comes through the raised voices—a quiet sound of fear and pride clashing under fake daylight. Her reflection in the glass looks like a ghost caught between two worlds—the harsh rules here and the softness she still wants.

"You're scared of losing your legacy," she says quietly. "But I'm scared too. Of becoming just another part of a machine, waking up and not recognizing myself. Your world doesn't allow feelings—it smooths them down, makes them obey. I can't lose who I am, not again. I fought too hard for this." Her voice shakes but is strong, even as she looks smaller.

The silence feels heavy—breaths uneven, both caught between fight and giving up. Rain hits the window behind Seraphina, breaking the city into strange shapes. Caius stands still, jaw tight, but a soft look crosses his face. He sees not just anger but fear—a mirror of his own.

How many times has he thought about letting himself fall apart? The Drakes never fall apart. The club never forgives weakness. But looking at Seraphina, something weakens inside him. Her honesty is sharper than any betrayal he has faced.

They stay like that, frozen in breath and doubt, the room full of old pain and new truth. The glass office quiets again, the city a faint beat below. For the first time, they both feel that to survive here, they must show the things they've always hidden.

The city spreads below, a sea of lights breaking the dark—a map of dreams beneath the top floor of Drake Investment Empire. Glass walls shine with unspoken words. The LED lights in the office are bright and cold, shining on Caius, revealing the tension after their fight.

Caius breathes slowly, standing stiff against the doubt inside him. For years, power was strength and intuition, sharp like a knife—but now, the city feels less like an empire and more like the edge of a cliff. Still feeling raw from the argument, he moves away from the desk, the silence tight and private. The cold floor is beneath his shoes. He steps toward Seraphina, fighting the urge to hide behind his usual walls; his jaw tight from the struggle to stay calm.

"I need you to listen," his voice is low and steady. "Your ideas—the ones you fight for—they haven't just kept us alive. They are the force behind what we've built lately. I—" He stops, his perfect words breaking. "I've begun to trust them. To trust you. Making decisions alone isn't what the firm needs. It's not what I need. Not anymore."

Seraphina listens quietly, her face reflected in the dark glass—part woman, part shadow above the city lights. Light shines in her chestnut hair, pulled back defiantly. Past fights left wounds on their trust: every battle in the boardroom carved doubt into their daily lives. But now, some of that doubt eases. She steps closer to the desk and lays her hand on the smooth wood, fighting the small shake left by fear and adrenaline.

"You want me to stand with you, not behind you." Her voice is low, full of serious courage from fighting for her freedom among powerful people. "If I stay—if I give everything I have—I won't lose my values. I won't trade myself for your empire. I'll fight with you, but I won't disappear into the walls you built." Her hand stays on the desk before she takes it away, a quiet promise.

He listens, respect showing in how he stands. He knows the language of strongholds—all edges, defenses, walls built to survive secret fights and planned betrayals. The old ways crack as Seraphina offers her help and stands firm.

He nods, silently accepting her terms. Together, they move to the window, side by side now. The city's angry hum beats through the glass: alive, relentless, a reminder that real problems wait outside these steel walls. Caius puts his hand on the cold window and looks out. A new strength shines in his eyes—not from power, but from something quieter and more dangerous: hope.

"You won't disappear," he says, his voice stronger. "Your voice stays, or none of us can win. Tomorrow, we face the senior staff together. The old way—the endless fight for control—almost cost me everything tonight."

Seraphina exhales, her tension easing as she joins him. Their reflections in the glass are no longer enemies, but partners—equal, determined, shaped by fire, not by contracts or reports.

They share a silent moment, full of thanks mixed with the pain of past losses, belief clear in their faces. Each nod, each look says: You matter here. Our weaknesses count. The moment feels fragile, like thin glass, shaped by the quiet hum of air vents and a siren echoing through the city.

For years, Caius kept secrets, afraid to share his burden—scared that the weight of his family's expectations would break him. He is still learning that power is not being alone, that true strength comes from shared risk and honesty. The office still feels foreboding, but tonight he allows fragile trust to hold him.

Next to him, Seraphina shakes off old pain—the ghosts of past betrayals, the hard-won freedom fought for in lonely studios and late nights. Their alliance is more than a plan; it is an act of creating together, a rough sketch for a world where power also has space for disagreement and care.

The city goes on, bright and dangerous. In this glass bubble above it, Caius and Seraphina stand together—quiet, steady, not because they are sure of everything, but because they respect each other and carry a new, stubborn hope.

Sunrise fills the glass walls of the Drake Investment Headquarters, casting golden light over empty streets below. On the high floor, a conference room awakens from quiet darkness, light pouring over shiny chrome and a polished wood table. Here, every surface shines, as if the room itself could keep away doubt—but this is only a hope, quickly broken by Caius Drake and Seraphina Hayes.

Caius leads, his steps light on the cold marble floor. He puts down stacks of folders carefully: 'Internal Risk,' 'External Threats,' 'Staff Problems'—each a sign of trouble hidden beneath the calm surface of the empire. His suit reflects the harsh light, but nothing softens the hard shadow on his face or the worry in his eyes.

Seraphina comes in softly, holding a tablet full of bright ideas and quick notes, some sure and some unsure. The room smells clean and cold—high-rise air kept fresh by filters and dreams. She looks out over the city, her shoulders steady, but the memory of last night's fight still hangs in the air.

Caius speaks first, his voice calm but firm. "We are weak. The board thinks someone is trying to harm us from inside. Our security is not just out of date—it's leaking. Two breaches came from inside accounts, one from new creative software." His hand moves over the folders, as if to protect them or himself.

Seraphina turns on her tablet, the screen showing bright colors like sunrise. "If you fix the holes by cutting the weakest parts, in three months the creative teams will be gone. They're scared. They talk about being emptied out. Design loses more people than accounts, and that's not random. Fear spreads. My team won't stay loyal if you watch their every move. They need to feel like they own part of this. Give them that, and they'll fight for you."

Caius raises an eyebrow, holding back doubt. "Innovation means nothing if the base is breaking. There is a sickness—disloyalty grows in secrets. If we don't get rid of it, everything will fall." He flips through reports: charts, warnings, filters of data.

"They are not disloyal. They are scared. People fight for places they believe in." She slides the tablet forward; colorful ideas bloom—plans for team design sprints, mentoring programs, employee spotlights with fun designs. Her finger traces paths between ideas, building a network between survival and new creation. "Let them build something—for the company, for themselves. Give them ownership, Caius, and the shadows lose power."

He pauses, and the silence buzzes with the weight of last night's truth. Betrayal has always been familiar: first at home, then in boardrooms full of fake smiles, always leaving trust broken bit by bit. Caius sees sabotage in every new worker's eyes. But here, Seraphina's strength is a light, breaking cracks in his wall of doubt.

He opens a notebook, writing quick plans: more security layers, staff training on cyber safety, ethical firewalls. But he also copies Seraphina's ideas beside these. Something about this—turning cold strategy into a web of people and hopes—feels hard but right.

She draws a mind map, lines moving from 'Risk Control' to 'Recognition Programs,' weaving through threats and hopes. Her pencil blurs the edges of old rules on the clean table, and Caius doesn't stop her. He listens, torn between wanting control and wanting to work together.

"You think your world is only steel, glass, and numbers," Seraphina says, not judging, just stating a fact. "But deep down, what will save you isn't stronger locks. It's people feeling they matter. Show them they are not just pawns."

He meets her eyes, his voice almost bare. "I will. Starting now. I will protect your ideas from the board and from too much red tape. You have my support and protection from interference." He glances at an intercom. "Tell my assistant to set up a meeting with all departments. Today. I want everyone involved, not just compliance experts."

Seraphina nods, her resolve matching his. Between them, the old walls of wounds and mistrust slowly break—not gone, but thinner from crisis and the need for something real.

Last night's fight still hums beneath everything: fear of failure, the sting of betrayal, the lonely climb to power. Caius has learned that fortresses that keep harm out also keep warmth away. But now, surrounded by glass and his own limits, he finds that giving up some control feels less like losing and more like making room for survival. For partnership.

Sunlight moves across the table, glinting on metal edges, catching the slight shake in Seraphina's fingers as she puts down her pencil. The city hums with hidden dangers, but here, for a moment, their alliance is stronger than fear.

Caius closes the last folder. Seraphina meets his gaze, the world outside vast and full of unknowns. This is not victory or peace. It is a fragile hope—an open hand, a chance to face the coming storm together.

Into the Fire

The war room glowed with cold, bright light that made faces look thin and eyes sharp. Glass walls showed every reflection and shadow, dividing the space like the strong ambitions of the people inside. Rain hit the windows, making the quiet feel even deeper as Caius entered with calm steps. His presence was tense—tight jaw, sharp suit, and guarded gray eyes.

At the center of the table, glowing blueprints of broken digital systems and hacked files hovered above the polished wood—reminders of what was supposed to be secure. The city outside blinked with neon lights, its tall buildings hiding cold and complex battles. Drake Investment Empire: strong in name and structure, but used to being attacked. The screens displayed facts and numbers: last night's secret report leaked to the press; market shares lost in precise strikes; alliances breaking like thin ice.

Caius placed his hands on the table, fingers steady, voice firm. He named the attacks and listed betrayals both old and new. Evidence appeared: times, access points, patterns—someone inside the company was working with the enemy, following unknown rules. He spoke of the saboteurs like predators: rivals inside the firm, connected to the Orion Club, twisting loyalty into deals. He warned—being exposed in this city means death, and no building can protect you from threats meant to destroy from within.

Some executives showed fear—knowing their wealth and pride were at risk—but most hid it behind practiced calm. Power in New York is a harsh game. Outside, alliances can disappear in a day, old deals replaced by leaked secrets, and even the walls might spy to gain an advantage. Everyone in the room understood one thing: holding power requires constant effort and is always in danger.

Seraphina leaned forward, flanked by Marcus's careful watch and Olivia's cautious stance. She asked to speak—not out of respect, but as a challenge. Caius nodded; her sharp eyes quickly scanned the screens.

Her clear words cut through the tension. "The leaks aren't random. Whoever is doing this plans each one for maximum damage. There's a pattern—the timing between outside attacks and inside data theft almost matches, as if someone is controlling the chaos on both sides."

She showed layers of digital traces: access logs hidden inside others, rewritten subprograms. She laid out a timeline—each hit on the company happened at the same time as small market gains for rivals, some linked to Orion. She suggested counterplans like an artist preparing a new canvas: watch for digital traces, bait the next attack, spread false rumors to confuse the enemy. Her voice was confident, with a hint of defiance—refusing to be ignored or erased.

Caius felt a headache growing, the familiar weight of responsibility pressing down. Control was everything to him; he had crushed rivals and emotions under it. But watching Seraphina, something cracked. She revealed threats with a sharp intuition like his own. He was frustrated at losing his usual certainty but also grudgingly impressed.

The discussion broke into pieces and came back together, shifting to Seraphina's new way of thinking. For more than an hour, they planned a response: legal moves, media campaigns, digital walls. Caius led with quick orders, but his tone changed to match Seraphina's pace—her plan for when to tell the press and how to defend in real time. He saw his empire bend to this outsider's ideas, and it unsettled him more than the attack did.

Seraphina said, "That third breach doesn't fit with the others. There's a delay, as if they waited for permission before moving."

"Which means what?" Caius asked sharply.

"It's not just a hired attacker. Someone close to us is running this. We could give them false information, watch which rival uses it, and then track what happens."

"And if we act too soon?"

"We don't. We let them think they won. Then we take control of the story."

Marcus, near the main console, broke the silence. He praised Seraphina's calm and added a new angle—the old Orion ties still mattered. His deep, steady voice reminded everyone that in New York, power depends not just on money but on secrets shared in private rooms.

Looking from Caius to Seraphina, he said, "Your work is sharp and fast. Keep it up. Use what the old ways offer, but don't underestimate fresh ideas."

Olivia nodded quietly, approving. The room's fear turned to focus. The threat was real, but now they moved forward together—an alliance no one expected just hours before.

Caius said, "We all know what's at risk. We do this tonight. No more leaks. No mistakes."

Marcus whispered, just for Caius and Seraphina, "You two are unexpected but already changing the game. Let them underestimate you."

Caius ended the meeting firmly. The leaders left, feeling the weight of what lay ahead. Seraphina stayed behind, her bright eyes in the room's artificial dawn. Caius met her gaze—an odd balance growing between them, born not of trust but shared challenges.

The quiet in headquarters felt heavy, like the calm after a storm. Caius led Seraphina down a hallway lit with soft teal light. Carpets absorbed their steps. At the hall's end, a glass door slid open softly. The lounge beyond was wrapped in dark shadows with warm gold lamps, softened by fine design. A slender bar glowed faintly, crystal glasses reflecting light on polished surfaces.

Caius poured himself whiskey, neat—the color deep like warm honey, the glass heavy in his hand. For Seraphina, he found her choice—dry red wine with earthy and berry notes. The cork pulled, and wine flowed quietly into the glass. These small rituals offered comfort in a world where comfort was rare and never guaranteed. Sitting on a leather sofa with a wide window in front, they watched the city's glowing streets below, like rivers of amber, silver, and neon blue. Above, the night sky was dark, occasionally lit by lightning between skyscrapers.

Rain ran down the window, blurring the city's reflection into something unclear. Seraphina held her glass, eyes tense, as if waiting for a hit. Her knee bounced once, then stopped. The silence wasn't cold, just cautious—two people from different worlds quietly noticing each other from the safety of shared darkness. Thunder rumbled, making the window shake.

She sipped slowly, the warm wine giving her courage that her heart lacked.

"This place," Seraphina said with a slightly shaky voice, "is built to wear you down. I know because I've felt it before." She looked away, watching raindrops fall. "Every step you take, someone wants to control or erase it. Even me. Tonight, I remembered all the times I spoke up and my ideas were ignored until someone else took credit. That was before—other jobs, other places—but the fear is the same." Her thumb touched the inked rose on her wrist, a painful memory. "I need you to know I won't let that happen here. Not now. Not with you."

The wine tasted sharp and full. Her words weren't drama—they were survival, shaped into a promise strong enough to hurt if ignored.

Lightning flashed, lighting Caius's face briefly. He held his whiskey without drinking, knuckles tight on the glass. He watched Seraphina for a long moment, weighing risk like a business deal—only feelings don't follow logic. He was good at protecting himself, finding control out of chaos since betrayal taught him not to trust. Now, under her steady gaze, his defenses felt thin, almost broken.

He sighed, shoulders dropping as if giving in. His voice was low and rough. "You think you're the only one trying to stay afloat?" He shifted, finally taking a burn from his drink. "Every room I enter, I have to control it, or someone else will. That's how it's always been. After what I've been through—after the last time I let someone close—it became the only way to live. I doubt, second-guess, keep secrets." Lightning lit a scar above his brow, making it shine. "But you... you don't play by my rules or anyone else's. I see how you change the mood, how people listen. I thought that would threaten me. Maybe I wanted to push you away. But you're not a threat. You're—" The word came slowly, carefully. "A challenge. And I don't want to stop that, even if control is all I know."

Seraphina swallowed. The storm pressed in, as if the sky was waiting for her answer. The space between them buzzed, fragile like the calm before a storm breaks. For the first time, her hand hovered halfway toward his, uncertain.

Caius set his glass aside. In the quiet, he reached out, covering her hand with his, warm and gentle. Her fingers tightened at first but then relaxed, finding his. Their hands formed a fragile bond, mixing surprise and hope under the storm's quiet drum.

No words came, just their breathing and the far-off roll of thunder. The city stretched below, large and indifferent. Caius felt sudden softness, something new—not defense, but openness.

Seraphina leaned back, tension melting into the sofa. The sharp anxiety eased; she could taste hope—new and untested, but real. Caius sat beside her, silent and still, letting the moment last. Lightning lit the skyline one last time, painting their faces briefly with honest light. In the quiet space, with the world and its dangers held back by glass and trust, a new, careful hope took root.

Morning filled the glass walls of the main conference room. Sunlight broke into soft gold across the polished black table. The New York skyline sparkled—tall buildings, flying vehicles, flickering light ads. Inside, the air was tense. Every seat at the table was full. Faces showed tiredness from the night's crisis, shoulders drooped slightly, digital tablets shifted, fingers tapped screens.

Caius sat at one end, sitting straight and sharp. He pointed out strategies on the room's digital display. He spoke clearly and with short sentences. He wanted to hit back fast against Pierce Equity—a rival company. His plan: legal actions, smearing their name, spreading rumors to damage their market position. He looked around for agreement. Older leaders—Olivia, sharp-eyed; Marcus, calm and serious—exchanged cautious looks. The room felt charged, as if the world itself was listening.

Seraphina stood across the table, hands steady on the glass edge. The air tingled softly as she interrupted with a clear, strong voice: "I have to disagree." All eyes turned to her—Olivia's brow raised, Marcus blinked in surprise, and junior staff watched eagerly.

Seraphina's presence changed the mood. She remembered old projects where her advice was ignored or wiped out by louder voices. Those times left marks but also strength, teaching her to stand firm no matter the cost. She took a deep breath, smelling faint heat and city stone through a cracked window, and spoke again. "We won't win by sinking to their level. If we escalate, we bring more public attention and hurt our team's morale. There are better ways. We should be open and control our own story. Here, reputation matters more than quick wins."

Caius crossed his arms, jaw tight. His cold stare showed his experience. "Being open sounds good, but our world is about attack and defense. If we hesitate or show weakness, rivals will destroy us. I've seen what waiting costs." His voice held years of betrayal. "Holding back is weakness."

Seraphina didn't flinch. She saw his calculation—the pain hidden behind his strength. But she also knew the hidden costs: losing team loyalty and creativity when people fear sudden attacks. "Respectfully, Caius, it's not just about enemies. When we fight back hard, it sends a message inside too. People are burned out. They watch every move, worried about layoffs and blame. My data shows aggressive moves lead to more staff quitting, less market trust, and more market ups and downs. That's not just numbers—that's us weakening ourselves."

A quiet fell—heavy and restless. Seraphina felt the mood shift. She saw it in a junior analyst's open mouth in silent agreement, Marcus's relaxed shoulders, Olivia's narrowed eyes, and the way her hand hovered over her stylus but didn't argue. This wasn't her old world, but she knew its rules—and was changing them, slowly but surely.

Caius's glare softened, suspicion turning to thought. He looked around the table, reading the unspoken signals. "Any thoughts?" His usual command softened into a real question.

Marcus nodded slowly, voice low but firm. "Seraphina makes sense. This is the first new way to handle a crisis we've heard in months. People watch us change power's rules—let's not waste that chance acting like before." A few others nodded in silent agreement, breaking the usual chain of command. Olivia spoke carefully, "A measured way doesn't show weakness. It might buy us time—and trust."

Their words turned stillness into motion. Seraphina saw the faces—Olivia now curious, Marcus's quiet promise, younger workers watching her with hope instead of doubt. She felt the shift—it was small but real. She doubted the respect would last forever, but today her words shaped not just moods but policy.

The meeting ended. Caius's face showed a brief, faint smile, but his eyes stayed narrowed and thoughtful. As others left, he caught Marcus's eye and motioned him down a nearby hall. Glass doors closed softly behind them.

"This is new," Caius said quietly. "She's useful. More than I thought. Did you see them? They respect her. It feels different."

Marcus's lips curved almost into a smirk. "Don't fear change, Caius. Sometimes the next step isn't force but hearing the right voice."

Seraphina left to nods and approving looks from colleagues. The glass room reflected her strong outline against the wide city. Not an outsider this time—not a pawn. Something new and sharp, noticed by all. Alone, Caius stood by the glass, watching the endless city. This time, when power shifted, he didn't fight. He just watched the sunrise bring the next challenge.

The Thorn Amongst Roses

Heavy velvet curtains separate the lounge from the outside world, blocking most sounds except for quiet footsteps on Persian rugs and the soft hum of men accustomed to power and wealth. Wall lamps cast warm, yellow light on the rich wooden walls, shining through a haze of cigar smoke. Beyond the leather sofas and the bar stocked with rare drinks, Damien Pierce enters, his presence palpable in the smoky air filled with whiskey and tobacco.

People watch him as he walks in, sensing a small but clear change in the room's energy. Damien sits at the head of the table, the leather chair creaking beneath him, his boots firmly planted on the floor. Three older members—Victor Harrington with gray hair, Alexander Chen with sharp eyes, and the quiet Russell Danforth—nod to each other. The fourth, Marcus Blair, younger and eager, sits straight, alert.

Damien looks around the table, allowing the silence to grow—it's an old routine in a windowless room full of secrets. This is not a normal club meeting. Beneath the city's grandest hotel, these men hold real power. They belong to an elite group that values tradition, secrecy, and control. Everything in the room, from the curtains to the carved furniture, serves as a reminder of who they are—and who others are not.

He clears his throat, halting the soft jazz music and the clinking of ice. Damien's voice is calm and confident, shaped by years of business meetings: "Gentlemen, recent changes in leadership necessitate a serious discussion. I hope you've all considered Caius Drake's new policies—and what might happen if this continues."

No one answers right away. The smoke fills the air like secrets. Finally, Victor Harrington speaks, his voice strong: "We've maintained this power for generations. This club is a bastion of strength—steady and firm. The ideas Caius brings—empathy and inclusion—are not part of our tradition. They threaten what we protect. Kindness and charity won't save us. Exclusion is what holds us together."

Alexander Chen keeps his eyes down but speaks sharply: "Caius is squandering what took centuries to build. He forgets what makes us different. If leadership weakens, cracks will show everywhere. We aren't a safe place—we shape the city's future. If he weakens us, our enemies will destroy us."

Damien's fingers tap slowly on the chair's armrest as he listens. Tradition is not merely looking back—it is protection, a force that keeps outsiders confused and afraid. The club is a secret circle, making decisions by ritual, not votes. Damien feels torn: should he uphold the old ways or open the door to changes that could ruin everything? His ambition battles his caution, loyalty contends with survival.

He leans forward. "Then perhaps we must act. Not tomorrow—now." His words are soft but firm. "If we don't stop this, what will be left? We'll be just another charity dinner club—weak and forgotten. We need to explore our options: alliances, voting if Caius persists, even secret surveillance. Our strength lies in unity, but unity won't last if it fades."

Blair speaks first, eager: "Do you really think Caius has lost it? He wouldn't change without reason. Someone's pushing him—perhaps someone from outside." He glances at the empty chair representing those not present—those who might be removed for the first time.

Victor laughs sharply. "He's blinded by emotions. That's how it starts. We must not be soft. We've faced rebellions before, but now the city wants to see weakness. Every day Caius falters, our enemies grow stronger."

Damien lets the words sink in, breathing in smoke and fear hidden behind pride. The city above believes its order is strong, but everything here influences government, money, and history. One leader's mistake could unravel it all. The others see Caius's changes as threats, but Damien feels the danger personally. Has he climbed so far only to watch it all fall for a cause he doubts? Loyalty, ambition, and survival all pull at him.

He lowers his voice, drawing them closer. "We need a reckoning. Let's meet with the veterans who understand why we exist. We'll make our stance quietly. Caius won't tighten control without us acting."

The room grows quiet. The smoke seems to hold still, listening. The murmurs fade into tense silence. Damien looks at the walls lit by flickering lamps, every shadow watching as their power shifts again. The club's future depends on their next move.

Marcus walks from the quiet corridor, his polished shoes silent on marble. He passes a security panel and closes the glass door behind him. Caius's office is cool and still, lit by city lights stretching outside. Caius stands by the window, tall and stiff, his suit sharp like the office's chrome and dark wood. Evening light brightens the scar above his brow. He doesn't turn, but Marcus sees the tension in his shoulders and jaw—he fights silent battles.

The city's noise below is distant—a machine always running, always needing more decisions and sacrifices.

"Caius," Marcus says softly, stepping into the room.

Caius continues to gaze at the city as if he can control it by will. "If you're here to stop me from ruining everything tonight, it's too late," he says dryly, fists clenched white. "They met under the hotel. They pretended respect, but it's all fake. Damien calls it tradition—as if tradition isn't just ghosts chaining us to the past."

Marcus moves carefully, stopping at the desk. "You know the city doesn't change quickly. If you confront the club tonight, you'll play by their rules. You risk breaking the alliances we've made. Even a wounded beast waits for the right moment."

They both pause—tension hangs between stubbornness and calm. Below, traffic moves like glowing rivers. Caius turns away and paces, the sound of his shoes soft on stone.

"It's foolish to think holding back protects me, Marcus. I showed weakness, and now they've gathered the old guard, whispering about legacies and danger—that I am weakening the club. Damien hides behind riddles but challenges me. I wanted new ideas, new blood. But any softness I show, they use against me. I'm not ruling in my father's shadow. I must build my own legacy—but they close in."

Marcus's voice is calm but strong. "You will build it. But not by openly fighting your own. Some people aren't fully on either side. Push too hard, and they'll join tradition—just what Damien wants. Speak quietly, and they'll stay with you, even if unsure. Keep your enemies guessing, and your friends—you keep your friends."

Caius stops pacing, listening beneath his doubts. The high office should excite him but feels heavy. His tired reflection looks back at him from the window: eyes worn, face tight with sleepless thought, the city's endless motion reflected where vulnerability peaks through his armor.

He wonders—what if he really opened the door? Trusted patience and let some things pass without fighting back? Would the club break apart, with the most loyal plotting against him? Or would people remember calm as real strength, something the old guard never saw?

He imagines leading not by striking harder but by standing firm, letting the enemy's attacks fall harmless. Would that bring respect or only tolerance? Would he be remembered or merely warned about as a leader who lost control? He fears being alone—the way power always isolates.

But hearing Marcus's steady support, neither harsh nor weak, gives him hope. Quiet alliances, respect earned by patience, not show. Could that change the club, shape it anew—his way?

Marcus reads him like a book, scarred but strong. "This is the cost, Caius. You asked for this burden. Every leader carves their own path. But if you hold to your values, if you don't back down, you can be more than feared—you can be followed."

Caius thinks this over, feeling both tired and hopeful. Marcus places a steady hand on his shoulder—a strong, grounding touch.

Caius looks up, breathing in the cool light. For a moment, he lets his guard down, trusting that he is not alone. Marcus's grip is a promise—silent but firm. The world below spins wild and unyielding. Here, at the top, patience is the bravest choice left.

Golden doors open as Seraphina enters, her blue satin dress causing whispers among the crowd. The ballroom shines with gold and cream colors. Light from huge chandeliers spreads in rainbows. Candle flames flicker on silver stands, filling the air with wax and floral scents. The room quiets slightly when she walks in—guests pause, sensing something has changed.

At the entrance, a security guard scrutinizes her gold-embossed invite. She feels his hard gaze and hears quiet judgments from others waiting. A lone violin plays above the background music. Beyond the velvet rope, the city's elite gather—shiny shoes, sparkling cufflinks, voices rising and falling like power itself.

Seraphina breathes in the scent of expensive perfume, old brandy, and hidden nervousness. She moves forward, shoulders set, knowing the tattoo on her wrist signifies a small act of defiance in this world of strict rules. She passes a group of women in silk, their jewelry glinting as they appraise her. Their eyes are hard, disbelieving, a tiny sneer when they meet hers. Their conversation quiets as she walks by.

"Impossible to think the club would accept someone so... different," hisses a woman in green.

"She's come far, but not from our world," a man says nervously, fiddling with his lapel—each word echoing the old stories behind these walls. Their voices fade like snow on glass.

Seraphina's cheeks flush, but she holds her head high. She feels every thread of her dress, the cool weight of borrowed pearls, her heartbeat. This place tests those who don't belong, often breaking them.

Near the grand piano, shiny and black, Victoria Ashcroft waits. Elegant and relaxed, Victoria smiles with a touch of sharpness, her hand covered in rings brushing dust from the keys.

"My dear, you're the talk of the night," Victoria says, her voice just above the music. "To see someone with such a refreshing background at our gala. We love authenticity, as long as it's not too obvious."

Seraphina's heart races, but she responds coolly. "Funny, Victoria, how 'authentic' only counts when you fit in."

"But tradition brings comfort. We all want harmony. Do you enjoy being here among old friends?" Victoria's eyes drop, staring at Seraphina's tattoo like a snake.

"I value honesty," Seraphina replies, firm and clear. "I prefer company that values people beyond family or invites. If I make you uneasy, perhaps it's not me who doesn't belong."

The room's noise falters—conversation stops, eyes fixate. Candlelight shines on her face as she meets Victoria's gaze. The old rules tremble, straining under their own outdated logic.

Victoria's smile fades.

A soft cough and the rustle of cloth signal Margaret Lang approaching. She says nothing but nods—a quiet sign of support. Behind her, a young woman looks at Seraphina with awe and encouragement. A man by the wine raises his glass slightly, then disappears into the crowd.

Seraphina feels the space grow slightly larger in that quiet moment—she senses the fine line between being excluded and barely accepted. This place is built to keep power safe, where every look and word is a test. The social order changes moment by moment, shaped by those brave enough to speak up.

She feels some eyes turn to her—some still cold, but others curious, a few with newfound respect. The orchestra starts again, violins and cello weaving the tension back into soft music. Light bends and shines around her. For a moment, her heart aches under her calm. She stands strong, aware of what she risks: being different, being seen, risking everything to be true.

Her power doesn't come from family ties, but from refusing to give in. She knows this courage might isolate her more—might make her a spectacle, not an equal. But in Margaret's nod and the subtle signs from younger guests, she finds hope. It's not full belonging yet, but proof that even here, change can slip in through tiny cracks.

She relaxes her shoulders and keeps looking forward as rumors and guesses swirl around her. The golden room hums with possibility. Tonight, standing apart might be its own kind of revolution.

The Edge of Vulnerability

Caius walks quietly through his fortress. The glass doors close softly behind him. Below, the city stretches out in countless lights—each one a hope, a risk, a piece of someone else's dream. He forgets the elevator's ding as his shoes tap on the polished marble floor. His steps are steady and serious. The office is clean and cool, with a faint smell of machine oil. He places his briefcase on the desk, the leather making a soft sound. Standing still, he looks out through the huge glass window.

The city spreads before him—a pattern of shapes and bright lights, filled with unseen purpose. Tall buildings shine like giants. The dusk cuts the skyline in dark blue and silver, bathing the city in cold, artificial twilight. The glass wall feels like both a shield and a stage. His empire spreads out, untouchable, but the steel and view only make him feel emptier inside.

He sits in a leather chair that fits him perfectly, still and straight. The quiet hum of his laptop fills the room. Files appear on the large screen—details, numbers, plans, reports marked in colors and logic. He scrolls and judges investments far away, but he can't focus on profit or loss. His sharp eyes soften, his pupils move, and his attention breaks as the numbers blur.

Memories creep into the neat order: Seraphina's steady gaze across a shiny boardroom table, unimpressed, as if she could see through his calm face. Her laughter from a café—a warm sound cutting through brick walls and soft sunlight, unlike the cold here. Her hand lightly touched his, briefly and without warning, a raw connection that stays with him despite the world of money and control.

He cannot calculate this. He pushes the laptop away. The desk is clean again—only his restless hands remain, and the faint white scar above his eyebrow is reflected in the glass. He looks up, catching the blue evening light, and presses his thumb on the old mark.

His mind rolls back—broken moments in time—to the night he got that scar; the pain, the heat, and his fierce refusal to show it. The lesson in his skin: weakness lets others take advantage; it breaks the legacy he fights for. All his life, he has chosen control, logic, and the fear of betrayal. But now, Seraphina's memory grows quietly, slowly breaking down his inner defenses. He hears her voice—bold and bright—while his own is cold and controlled. He tastes coffee and sugar on her skin; he knows she is changing this safe place.

He closes his eyes, thumb still on the scar. For a moment, the city noise fades, and only his pulse remains. The office is safe, but inside him, something is unprotected. He wonders—what if he lets himself feel this longing, drops his guard, breaks the rules? It seems crazy. Dangerous. But the thought won't go away: maybe connection isn't weakness, but a door to something new.

The future stretches out, impossible but tempting—he imagines stepping beyond control, meeting Seraphina as she is, free and uncertain. In that future, his empire is different: not a fortress that blocks closeness, but a place for truth, even if it shatters his carefully built image. The fear is strong and sharp. He pictures freedom, mistakes, ruin—so many ways the world could take him down if he lets go. But hope stays alive under his skin, stronger than fear.

The LED light above glows like fake daylight, mimicking a sun long gone. His shadow blends with the city skyline: glass, steel, and single-minded purpose. He hates how much the office looks like his mind—perfect order, planned carefully. Isolation reflected in every clean surface. But his thoughts, wild and restless, won't follow these rules. They are filled with the shape of a woman who won't be tamed.

He sits silently, breathing slowly, surrounded by the distant city noise and the sharp smell of ambition. Beyond the office's perfect order and calm, Caius feels the chance of falling apart—of opening doors that can't be closed again. The choice gets closer, casting a shadow on the glass—unclear, inviting. For now, he stays by the window, staring into the quiet blue night, unable and unwilling to clear away what's coming.

The elevator moves up silently, smooth and quiet. Seraphina's heart beats louder in her ears. The steel walls shine with her reflection. Neon lights from the city flicker behind the glass. Her fingers grip her worn messenger bag, the soft fabric comforting—a reminder of a simpler world far below this high place. The elevator doors open gently onto a hallway filled with soft amber light. Caius's penthouse is big and sharp-edged, softened by the blue evening light outside the huge windows. Metal art, twisted into strange shapes, stands against dark glass walls. The silence is deep, broken only by the faint sound of the city far below.

She steps in carefully, her feet sinking into the soft carpet—each step deliberate, like crossing a border. Caius stands by the large window, his reflection mixing with the bright cityscape. He is both part of and separate from the world he rules. He doesn't turn when she enters, but they notice each other. The air smells faintly of sandalwood and cold steel.

"Seraphina," he says quietly, his voice slow and serious, almost like a shadow's voice. She stops just before the couch, deciding whether to cross the line.

"Evening," she replies, calm but firm, touching her bag strap to steady herself. "I finished the updated campaign for the sustainability project. I thought you'd want..." Her words stop as his eyes meet hers, sharp and unreadable like stars caught in black glass. In his gaze, she sees not just a boss, but a guard to something more dangerous.

He gestures, inviting but formal. She sits on the edge of the dark leather couch, ready to leave.

He moves smoothly but tired, like a weary hunter, and sits in the chair across from her. They face each other like two players caught between welcome and fear. The city lights stretch below, as if the night itself is waiting.

Their first words are stiff and formal: company projects, progress, numbers, deadlines—a script for a safer world. Between them is distance filled with purpose, not comfort. Every brush of her knee against the bag, every small movement of his body, is part of a careful dance.

Silence grows heavy. Caius's fingers rest on his knee, trembling slightly in the soft lamp light. When he finally speaks, his calm face cracks.

"I don't know if giving up some control," he says quietly over the city's night sounds, "will destroy me or set me free." He looks away, following rows of streetlights into the dark. "I have built walls so thick I wonder if anything human remains inside. You—you make me imagine what life would be like without them. That scares me. Maybe more than ruin or failure, because it could cost everything. The empire. My reputation. And something real with you, which is rarer than all of it."

His words hang between towers of money and power. Seraphina watches him, her heart skipping; her breath catches at his rare openness.

"I don't know how to live here," she says softly, her voice shaking with quiet strength. "Where kindness feels like a deal. I tell myself I can play their game and still be me, but—" She laughs without humor, pulling her knees closer. "I can't be a pretty distraction or fit their plan. If I lose myself, I have nothing left to give. I want to see what we can be, even if it scares me. But I won't ever apologize for who I am. Not for them, not for the club, not for you."

The city lights refract through the windows, casting broken gold across the room. Seraphina twists her bag's leather, small nervous movements that are a private shield. Caius's calm face slips; his jaw is tight, but his eyes soften, showing doubt and hope.

Between them, trust grows—not as certainty, but as a risk they both accept. Every beat, every look, is a careful step neither names.

The tension feels like a tight wire—both cautious but not cold. Beyond company goals and club politics, something wild now guides their words.

Caius feels the weight of his empire deep inside him, remembers loneliness and every betrayal and victory he faced alone. But now, under the calm of privilege, something wild stirs—reckless and unsure. He is both king and prisoner of his own fortress.

Seraphina sees possibility in risk. Her fierce but shaky will challenges every shadow in the penthouse. In this still moment, she is not stopped by doubt but surprised by it, holding stakes she never wanted but won't give up.

Neither speaks. Outside, the city shines, unreachable. Inside, silence is filled with breath, hope, and fear—waiting to see if trust can last long enough to be real.

The penthouse living room glows in the deep blue of the city night. The glass wall behind Caius and Seraphina shows New York's scattered lights—each a story heading toward a meeting or an ending. The world outside is alive: below, cars move and sirens call, energy flows through concrete veins. Inside, everything is simple and smooth: black marble, soft leather, silence so deep that even a soft sound becomes important.

A phone buzzes, breaking the stillness. Caius's phone lights up on the coffee table, glowing white-blue. The message is from Marcus. Just one line, but full of meaning: The club is breaking apart. Emergency meeting. Some will act tonight.

Caius's breath tightens. There is no space for doubt, yet it creeps in—the kind he knows from long nights at power tables, half-lit by secret fights. Years of boardroom games and the hidden rules of The Orion Club taught him that these moments never come alone. They carry ghosts of loyalty tested and knives hidden beneath polite words. He feels the old habit return—tight shoulders, sharp mind, the urge to bury feelings in facts.

But something fights back. Something new and raw. His recent secret feelings, Seraphina's words still fresh, make him nervous in ways no numbers can fix. Fear and hope coil inside him, pulling memories of old club troubles and the ruin that comes when empires—family, money, or feelings—start to fall apart.

He sets the phone down gently, as if it might explode. Seraphina sits beside him on the long leather couch, her shape lit by city glow and shadows. She sees the tension carve his face sharper, notices the tight jaw and clenched hand covering the phone screen. Her nerves jump—a shiver not caused by the room's temperature.

She leans slightly, reading his face. "Bad news?" Her voice is soft, her usual openness held back by the heavy mood.

He pauses. Training tells him to stay silent, but Seraphina's doubt, fear, and hope push him to speak. "The Club," he says. "Marcus says something is happening. They're breaking apart. They want me... now."

Her hand tightens on her bag strap, knuckles turning white as she swallows hard. "Because of tonight? Because of us?"

"It's more than us," Caius answers, his voice cold but near breaking. "But it's coming. Sooner than I hoped."

She leans back as if shocked, letting the bag rest on her knees. Her eyes travel down his arm to the scar above his eyebrow, reading the map of old wounds—some seen, some hidden—that shape how he moves. For a moment, she just breathes him in: the soft sandalwood scent, the sharp neatness of his space, the storm she didn't mean to start.

Neither moves. The small space between them feels huge—a gap made from broken dreams and worn trust.

Caius studies Seraphina, her face lit by the city's ghostly light. She looks strong but near breaking. He feels the same fear that tightens his veins in moments when stakes are higher than he can hide from. His old instincts from climbing the ranks of power—every look a threat, every ally fragile—meet a new desire: to protect, not fight; to take a chance, not build walls.

Each second grows heavy with possibilities neither says out loud. The emergency feels like a dark cloud, covering the penthouse with cold light and distant sounds. The walls seem to shine—not warm, but sharp and perfect—daring them to step out from their shields.

He shifts slightly to speak—but stays silent.

She breathes in and lets it out slowly.

The silence remains. Outside, taxis move like glowing bugs through neon canyons. Inside, only the soft touch of Seraphina's sleeve as her hand rests between them. Caius's hand mirrors hers—so close that moving could break or bind whatever fragile thing they share.

The space shrinks. Neither reaches out, but neither pulls away. In their quiet, something new begins—the storm is close, but for now, they wait side by side, breathless.

Flames of Change

Low amber light shines from fancy wall lamps, breaking the darkness in the Orion Club's boardroom. The polished mahogany table gleams, and silver trays with untouched drinks glint in the light, cold drops of water forming on them. The doors open and close quietly as one well-dressed person after another enters—shoulders straight under heavy wool coats, whispers hidden in their collars. Leather chairs creak as a group of powerful men and a few women take their seats—faces showing the confidence of old wealth, eyes sharp under the chandelier's glow.

The room grows quiet but tense. The smell of cigar smoke, carried away through hidden vents, mixes with cologne and cleaning polish—a reminder of old deals and long-held grudges. Quiet talks are sharp and quick: "Drake's taking risks," "Feeling over reason," "No room for weakness." The air feels heavy with doubt and the threat of hidden warnings. Long-standing traditions—strong rules of the Orion—hover just below the surface, kept alive by men who value power and not kindness.

Caius is the last to enter. His eyes are like storm clouds over a city. He moves slowly and carefully, taking his place at the head of the table—the city's ruler on his throne, face unreadable. No one misses the small twitch in his jaw or how his eyes briefly pass over Seraphina sitting at his right before looking back at the room with cold detachment.

Across the table, Damien Pierce stands, breaking the silence with the soft scrape of his shoes. His voice is strong and confident, shaped by years of leading instead of asking.

"There comes a time," he begins slowly and clearly, "when feelings are risks." He looks directly at Caius. "We respect tradition here. We value clear thinking. But lately, our leader has... wavered." His eyes scan the room for agreement. "Decisions influenced by personal matters—outside this room—have hurt our business."

He pauses to let his words sink in. "The deal with the Aurelian Fund. The delays in approving the Goodman purchase. The way some relationships look to the public." Damien's face stays calm, but his words challenge Caius quietly yet firmly. "The Orion isn't used to acting on impulse or emotion. It expects strong, focused leadership."

The room grows quiet again. All eyes turn to Caius—some calculating, some cautious, others ready to act. Damien's stare holds until heads slowly nod in agreement.

"Honestly, I wonder if personal feelings should ever get in the way of protecting our order. You should wonder too. Isn't that what this Club is about?"

"You talk like strategy never involved risk. Or did you only notice when it stopped working for you?"

Damien's lips press tight. "Risks are calculated. But this"—he gestures slightly toward Caius—"feels unpredictable."

Uncertainty spreads in the room. Some senior men whisper quietly. One, wearing shiny cufflinks, mutters, "He's right. The order is only as strong as its leader." Others shift, some uneasy, others challenging. Rivals exchange looks full of tension and hidden deals. The silver trays remain untouched; no one wants to risk loosening focus with a drink when every word could change the power balance.

Caius stands still like a statue, arms crossed, breathing steadily, his back straight against the judgment. His eyes appear calm on the surface, but inside, the room weighs heavily on him. Despite years of training and careful power-building, he feels a sharp pain beneath his skin: the memory of Seraphina's trembling hand earlier, the vulnerability in his confession. The Club's gaze doesn't burn him—it studies, looking for any sign of weakness. His grip tightens, fingers turning white. Showing doubt, anger, or kindness is forbidden here, yet the room's pressure pushes him to the limit.

He stands among them—a man caught between control and survival—and wonders if they see the cost. Tradition here is like a solid shell: perfect, suffocating, and unwilling to change. In this world, alliances break at the slightest sign of weakness, and affection is like a scent that attracts danger. Across the table, Marcus watches—a silent question in his eyes—waiting to see not if Caius is strong, but if he can survive what they expect.

"You've heard Damien," another voice says, tense with expectation, "but will our leader answer? We want clear thought. Confidence. Not complications."

Seraphina doesn't move. She is still, but the worry in Caius's eyes reaches her—his secret, fragile reason for not breaking down. Around them, voices rise, tension grows, the old members waiting for a show. Finally, silence falls. Everyone looks at Caius, and the weight of a hundred years of expectations threatens to crush him, even as he tries to seem as solid as those before him.

The silence deepens as Seraphina stands. Her body is straight and steady, dividing old tradition from the uncertain now—a figure with soft olive skin and strong posture moving through the leather-covered men of the city's secret rulers. The amber light highlights her cheekbones and the small shadow of a thorned rose on her wrist. She remains calm beside Caius, meeting Damien Pierce's eyes without fear.

The room feels heavy with old power—the smell of tobacco and sandalwood mixed into the carpets, heavy and unseen like an ancient story. Seraphina breathes it in and lets the strong taste settle, remembering her mother's words—Never shrink—etched deeper than ink. She notices every glance, how the men use their fine clothes and steady moves to hide from the unknown. Every pair of eyes sees her as an outsider, a challenge to the stability that keeps the city's glass walls from breaking.

When she speaks, her voice is clear and steady, like heated glass.

"No one here fears failure more than you fear the future. I hear it in every complaint and doubt. But you—" she looks at the group, landing on Damien—"are the ones building what comes next. Caius Drake has chosen honesty and vision over easy lies, and that is not weakness. That is what leaders do before history remembers them."

Damien's lips tighten, but he remains quiet. A small skeptical murmur comes from an old member, but it fades into the growing quiet. Seraphina stands strong, not pleading but pushing forward. She shares facts: profits rising after Caius's risky green-energy move, an international deal based on trust that gives the Club more influence. Each example builds the case she's making, showing tradition can survive not by holding to the past but by staying relevant.

"You ask for strength and vision. But you can't burn every bridge hoping old roads will still work. You want to keep the Club safe—fine. But what are you saving if you empty it because you fear change or one man's truth?"

"So honesty is your answer to decline?" Damien's voice is cold. "Or is it just a convenient excuse for mistakes?"

"It's the only real thing left when everything else is fake," Seraphina answers, her voice clear in the wood-paneled room.

The members exchange looks—some admiring, some uneasy. Some lean forward, hands near their mouths, considering her not just as Caius's voice but as an equal, or at least someone with her own stake. A young man, barely in his twenties, seems to see the room in a new way through her eyes. The older members sit back, hands tightening at the idea that power can change when a stranger stands at its center.

Her eyes find Marcus Langston—a steady presence, his face unreadable except for a small smile and nod, approving her step into this risky circle. His quiet support sends a subtle charge through the air.

Inside, Seraphina's heart beats fast. She tastes the risk and memory—her mother's kitchen, where hope was like fresh bread and sunlight, nothing like this room where honesty is suspicious. She stands not just for herself or Caius but for a future that must include her voice. Being an outsider is not a weakness; it is her strength and proof. And she feels the eyes testing if she belongs or could break their world.

What am I risking? she thinks, feeling tightness in her chest. Everything I wanted: respect without giving in, a seat at the table without becoming what the table demands. And hidden deeper—a hope Caius sees her not just as a protector but as a mirror for his own wish to believe change is possible.

She concludes, breathing steadily. "If you doubt him, if you doubt what got you this far, then you must doubt your own traditions. Because they allowed this. Me. Something new."

A heavy pause falls like snow on quiet streets. Eyes bounce between Seraphina and Caius, doubts softening, opening to something raw and uncertain. The room feels ready to change.

Caius's stiff posture eases, a soft tension around his mouth loosening as he meets her gaze. In his eyes is thanks and surprised respect. The power structure seems to shift, the old walls breathing, the air trembling—not with fear, but with a new beginning.

No one speaks. The room is still, caught in what she has made happen.

Caius Drake rests his palms on the smooth mahogany table. The cool wood steadies him as he takes deep breaths. Shadows move in the amber light of the Orion Club, covering every aging face around the table. Above, the chandelier throws golden circles that flicker over suits and glasses—lighting the silent wait, the careful poses, the practiced ignoring of fear. He feels all eyes on him, their judging gaze as sharp and cold as his own front.

The silence is quiet and tense, ready to break under the heavy weight of expectation in this place—a fortress built to stop doubt and keep power in the family. For generations, these walls have held secrets and deals—a test for the chosen, a trap for the careless. Caius's presence keeps the legacy alive, every move tied to ancestors whose portraits watch from dark corners. But now, there is a deeper weight—something restless, human, beneath the polished surface.

He breathes in, the faint smells of cigar smoke and fine cologne tickling his throat. For a moment, he is somewhere else—running on rooftops as a child, racing in the rain with his sister's laughter behind him, hair wet and free. That freedom is gone, banished by inheritance and duty. The room, despite the silence, hums with hidden plans and quiet threats. Every man here—each rival—thinks his armor is perfect.

Slowly, Caius steps away from the table, his body tight. For a moment, pride clings to him like a second skin; then, in the heavy gaze, it begins to crack and fall. He lets it go. The danger is real, rooted in rules as old as the city—show weakness, and the wolves attack.

He looks over the faces. Damien is already judging, waiting; Marcus is still, giving a small nod, a steady point in a sea of danger. Seraphina stands nearby, her hair like sunlight even in this dark room, her confidence a bright flame in the dark. Something about her shakes the strong walls inside him.

His voice is sharp and tired. "You want honesty?" His words don't echo; the thick tapestries swallow sound. "I have carried this burden long before I touched this chair. I know what is needed—the keeping up appearances, the careful moves, the constant dance of power." The old rules of the Club are unspoken but felt in every look.

His voice rises and breaks a little. "But the truth is, I falter. I'm not immune to the fear that every choice I make—every deal in this room—could bring ruin. That one mistake could break everything my family built, and I'd be left to face the ghosts."

A small tremor runs through the room; the glasses rattle softly, but no one moves. Caius's mask slips more, showing deep fears hidden beneath the city's bright surface. Eyes around him widen—some shocked, some feeling betrayed, others quietly noticing a new way of power.

"There are nights I can't sleep thinking that the standards set before me—by this Club, by my family—can't all be kept without losing something important. I've tried for years to think strength means silence, control means being untouchable," he says, his gaze moving as if speaking to the room and to his own troubled mind. "But that control almost cost me who I am."

He turns, looking briefly at Seraphina—an unbreakable link between them. Her eyes are steady; they offer no rescue, only challenge. In her, he finds a sharp truth that cuts deeper than the false pride here. "It was Seraphina who reminded me—through fight, through refusal—that being real and being strong are not the same as being weak. That holding on to your truth is a legacy worth building."

His next words ring clear and firm. "Maybe we don't need another generation of ghosts and puppets," he says, sharp but soft. "But leaders who are honest and strong. That is the future I want. That is all I have to offer."

The room feels the change like a spell. Silence stretches wide and bright. Some men frown, their faces showing confusion or anger. Others, including Marcus, show a quiet smile of approval. Damien looks at Caius with a hard, unreadable look, planning the next move. The old foundations seem to shift, unsure.

In the quiet, Seraphina steps closer, her presence holding the moment. Power is no longer a fortress or a show—it hangs between them, fragile and new. The Club's old rules wait, uncertain, its future changed forever.

New Dawn

Caius Drake walks onto the shiny stage, calm and confident. A small scar above his eyebrow tingles under the bright TV lights. Behind him, tall glass walls display New York's sharp skyline shining in the late-morning sun—a powerful city holding its breath. Journalists from various companies stand in careful lines. Cameras click, and microphones are held up like offerings to a new leader. People watch Caius with sharp, curious eyes. The Drake logo shines coldly on the screen behind him.

Next to him, Seraphina stands tall and steady. She looks strong in this steel-filled world: her chestnut hair pulled back, her face calm but determined. Their footsteps echo on the marble floor—two people, balanced in light and shadow. Many cameras flash, filling the glass with quick bursts of light. She doesn't blink. The air smells like coffee, metals, and new carpet mixed with the excitement of something about to happen.

Caius stops at the podium's curve. He takes a steady breath and grabs the microphone. His voice is sharp and clear. "Thank you for coming," he says, filling the room and breaking the tension. "I don't usually talk about personal matters in public. But today, I have to. I want to share something I've kept private for too long." He doesn't read from notes—the words are learned by heart, shaped by many sleepless nights. "Seraphina Hayes is my partner. In life, in spirit. And from today, in leading this company's future."

Journalists pause, unsure between manners and eagerness. Caius's words feel new and bold, mixing personal feelings with business in a way that surprises everyone. The room is silent, full of energy waiting for what comes next.

"We are not just partners in life," he says, "but also in our vision for Drake Investment. Together, we will change what leadership means today." His words break old ideas. Pens write quickly. Fingers tap phones, sending urgent updates. Seraphina stands beside him, head held high; her eyes look over the crowd but rest on him, showing support.

Questions come quickly.

"Mr. Drake, does this go against your own rules about mixing personal life with work?"

"Will Ms. Hayes take an official role—does this risk unfair treatment?"

"Do you expect anger from shareholders or The Orion Club?"

"Is this a sign of weakness or a new era of honesty?"

Some voices sound shocked, others respectful. The room buzzes as names, headlines, and hashtags spread on phones and screens. In this city, rumors are currency. In this web of power, media creates and destroys reputations, makers of kings and their falls. Every big news story here echoes outside: boardrooms change plans, rivals look for chances. An announcement is never just news—it predicts a future no one can guess. It shows a man once all about control now risking his heart in public.

Caius looks at Seraphina. Inside, he fights with his father's strict rules, club codes burned into his memory. Every part of him wants to protect himself, but he faces the moment. He breathes out, dropping his guard.

"Drake Investment will face challenges because of this," he says quietly, not for the crowd but for her. "I will face them. Risks to legacy, order, alliances—I accept them because I believe in something bigger than old power rules." Love and risk lay bare in front of bright lights. "I choose this, knowing I invite doubt. I refuse to be held back by fear or the past."

Seraphina touches his hand. The noise of cameras, signals sent everywhere, questions—none break their quiet strength.

"Will you resign if the board is against this, Mr. Drake?"

"Is this not a weakness—"

"Is this a model for secret relationships among the elite?"

Their voices fade as Caius turns, holding Seraphina's hand. They step away together into the storm, their linked images showing on screens across the city—no longer rumor but a new fact.

The Orion Club's private lounge is bathed in warm light, shadows stretching over rich woodwork and worn leather chairs. The room smells of old whiskey and faint cigar smoke, symbols of a world that loves both luxury and secrecy. Soft piano music fades under the low hum of breaking news on small screens—Caius Drake, distant and powerful, and Seraphina Hayes, the new partner, joined for all to see.

Damien Pierce moves quietly through the room, his polished shoes soft on thick rugs. His jaw tightens as he scans the room for signs of weakness in the group that has, for years, protected power from outside eyes. Damien stands alone near the bar, wearing a sharp suit like armor for a war of secrets. Conversations pause when he speaks.

"The real question," Damien says clearly, "is not about romance but about legacy." Glasses stop mid-hold; the room falls silent. "We know what happens when private matters affect business—our foundation cracks." Memories of past losses hit the group—Silas Carmichael, who broke the rules and lost everything to the press; Alvina Sorel, whose secrets brought legal troubles and fear. Damien looks around, daring anyone to disagree. "Leaders have risked empires on secrecy. They've fallen for less than what just happened on those screens."

In the dim light, memories fill the space between faces. Damien recalls a cold winter when a member's secret affair led to open investigations, breaking the club's long-held silence and traditions. To Damien, the club's power depends on its secrets. Loyalty and guardedness are defenses against chaos, built from fear and past pain, like when Caius once challenged him in a risky business deal that almost exposed them all. Old wounds throb as screens show headlines: "A New Era for Power: The Drake-Hayes Alliance."

Damien's doubt is not just personal. Every member here is both a rival and a possible partner, with shifting alliances. He notices Barrett in a corner wishing for Caius's fall, while Reiner listens, ready to side with the strongest voice. The club is like a many-headed monster, each part fighting to survive.

The doors open, and Marcus Langston enters, moving calmly. He commands quiet respect, earned through years of facing storms. Marcus looks at the group with steady poise. No show, just quiet confidence from experience.

"Change scares us all," Marcus says, his voice rich like the old whiskey in the room, "but stubbornness leads to obsolescence. We've survived wars, recessions, and scandals by understanding change." He looks at Damien. "We stay strong not by hiding, but by adapting. What you see on those screens isn't just risk—it's a chance to change power, not cling to fragile old ways."

"You speak of change, Marcus, but you have years to fall back on. What if this is the mistake that ruins us?"

"And what if it's the move that protects us for another generation?" Marcus speaks calmly, kindly. "Now we choose: stay stuck or grow."

Whispers spread around the room. Younger members quietly rebel; they see Caius as a brave leader or maybe a rebel testing old rules. The older members retreat, drinking quietly and holding private doubts. Barrett leans in, worried. Reiner watches greedily, weighing risk and reward. Loyalty here shifts fast like stock prices—uncertain and hungry for signs.

The air is still but heavy with unspoken worries, as if history itself watches. Glasses clink sharply, warning of trouble ahead, as the group breaks into smaller parts—old and new, loyal and eager—split along lines tradition can no longer hide.

Night darkens the tall windows of Caius Drake's penthouse office. The city below looks like a map of glowing dots and moving lights, like the veins of Manhattan. The glass desk shines under bright LED lights, but the room feels softer in the dark. Papers and digital files are spread across the desk: plans for change, ideas for openness, names of allies and opponents. Caius's silver watch catches the light as he moves his hands, calm but uneasy. His other hand rests near Seraphina's, the space between them full of quiet energy.

Seraphina sits opposite him, her wrist tattoo—a thorned rose—showing in the light. She leans forward, her eyes not on the skyline but on the list of names on the papers. Her breath nearly fogs the glass. She feels the weight of this room, this moment, like standing on the edge of a new era.

Caius breathes slowly. The papers seem to shift under his touch, as if moved by invisible forces.

The city's never-ending energy flows up to them through the glass and steel. Drake Investment's headquarters is not just a symbol of power but a fortress against uncertainty—a place built on secrets but now feeling change. News still plays softly in the background. In the elite world, public statements—especially about love—shake the old system. Names and legacies, balanced on old customs, can fall apart with one honest moment.

Caius points to the list of senior partners, his voice low and steady. He names those who resist change and those who might be won over by feelings, loyalty, or public opinion. Facing Seraphina, he offers her a pen—a sign to decide together.

"If we start with Marcus and Olivia, secure their support, and use the good feelings from the announcement... others might follow. But Winston will resist, and Lyle—if he senses weakness—will try to take advantage."

Seraphina traces a finger down the list, warm against the cool screen. "People respond to more than facts and rules. What if we show them our vision—not in dry statements, but in real work? Let them see a future they want, not one they fear."

"You know they'll call that sentimental. Weak." Caius's voice is firm, but his eyes soften as he looks at her.

She raises an eyebrow. "The old ways got us stuck—the same people making the same secret decisions. It won't last another decade. If they want to call hope fragile, let them. The world outside moves too fast for their old rules."

A quick, faint smile crosses his face, fading before it can be called a surrender.

Silence fills the room. The city lights below seem both ancient and new, showing a world where towers might crumble to nature. Power has always survived by changing. Still, in this quiet space, resistance hides: people holding onto old rules, wary of new ideas. Caius knows change can cause rebellion. He imagines secret talks, coded messages, centuries-old traditions not easy to break with speeches or love.

He weighs the risks like a tightrope walker crossing a big gap—one wrong step and everything falls. But Seraphina's presence steadies him. He feels the fear and strength in this moment, realizing vulnerability, once seen as weakness, might be the only way forward.

"We'll need friends outside the company too," Seraphina says quietly. "Artists, activists, people who believe change can be beautiful. They'll bring stories, design, and public support—mixing style and values."

"That's risky. I can protect you, but I can't promise the board won't strike back in some way."

"I'm not naive, Caius. You chose to risk everything for love, openly. I'm with you."

"I won't let them harm you," he says sharply. "Or the future we want. This company, these walls, my name—everything is at stake. For you. For our future."

She covers his hand, grounding him. "My values don't disappear under pressure. Fear won't define us. Together, we take the risk and set the rules."

He closes his hand gently over hers. For a moment, there is only the city below, endless and bright, the promise of new beginnings painting them clearly. Against the unknown, two people in a glass fortress begin their new story, brave and ready as the world watches.

Flames and Thorns

Night fills the penthouse suite with a soft, warm light from an overhead lamp. Caius and Seraphina sit side by side on a dark velvet sofa. Beyond the glass walls, New York's skyline shines with bright lights, the tall buildings standing like old guards with glowing crowns. The silence between them isn't empty; it feels full and thoughtful, like the city breathing against the window.

Caius leans forward, the soft sound of his wool sleeve moving as he picks up a heavy, cold glass. His reflection flickers in the glass—his sharp jaw, a small scar above his brow, and the light in his gray eyes. He hands the glass to Seraphina, being careful, as if the moment is more personal than expected. She takes it, her thumb brushing his hand quietly.

He sits back, looking past her to the glowing city. Her laugh breaks the quiet—soft and lively but gentle enough to maintain the calm. It reminds Caius of months ago when she would burst into his office after a bad pitch, daring him to argue with her. She taps the rim of her glass, catching specks of dust in the light, and smiles.

"Do you remember our first meeting?" she says. "You were exactly four minutes late and looked at my mood board like it was something strange."

He smiles slightly and exhales a dry laugh. "You told my directors, right in front of an expensive sculpture, that my color choices were 'lifeless.'"

"You said avant-garde can't mean 'chaos,'" she replies with bright eyes. "And I told you the art made me crave fire."

They laugh together, the sound rising to the ceiling where the lamp glows. Outside, car horns sound as the city hums with energy and hidden plans. For a moment, memories flow between them: sharp words in meetings, stolen looks during late nights, old ways clashing with new resolve until something changed.

"I didn't want to lose," Caius says quietly, his fingers moving along his pants. "I planned every word. But every challenge you made... made me doubt my defenses."

Seraphina watches him, bathed in the lamp's glow, holding her cool glass. "The way you looked through me that first week—like you saw everything but nothing mattered—made me angry. But it also made me wonder if anyone ever truly saw you."

The wind presses softly against the glass, a quiet hum. Under the city lights, memories connect past and present—Caius, always calm, learning to control himself around her; Seraphina, her fire mixed with curiosity, turning into something softer but more dangerous.

She moves closer until her knee touches his. The air feels full of hope.

"I need you to know—" Her voice shakes a little. "You have changed. Not just the company. You. I see it in how you let me in, even when it's hard, especially when you're scared. That means more than any deal."

She holds his hand tightly, as if steadying herself.

He pulls her close on purpose. When he turns to her, the city's lights reflect in his eyes—alive with hunger and pain. His hand covers hers, holding her steady. In that moment, his guard falls.

"Seraphina, I've lived believing control was the only way to avoid betrayal. That love and trust were weaknesses. But you..." His voice softens, almost reverent, his usual mask fading. "For you, I will fight. Not for power or legacy, but for what we build together. Whatever stands against us—whatever walls I must break—your place beside me is as important as the empire."

The city seems to agree. She rests her head on his shoulder, hands joined like survivors. Caius's thumb slowly strokes her finger, each movement a quiet promise.

Outside, the night grows darker, but inside, under the lamp and stars, calm grows. While the world outside moves with secrets and ambition, here in this mix of luxury and shadow, grief and hope, Caius and Seraphina live between fear and belonging, letting silence say what words cannot. The city beats below, and for once, they both believe their fortress and their flame can exist together.

A pale light spreads over Caius's glass and metal desk. He sits in his office with the city behind him. The morning sky is ghostly, dawn mixing with the dark blue shadows of skyscrapers. Caius wears a sharply cut suit that catches the small lights above, showcasing the power he commands and the armor he keeps. Seraphina stands by him, notebook open, finger marking sketches and notes—signs of a restless, focused mind. The air smells faintly of machine oil and citrus, leftovers from last night's late meeting. The city smells deeper—diesel, ambition, and longing.

Caius scrolls through news feeds on his tablet, which is quiet and smooth. Headlines shine on the glass: "Orion King's Heir Backs Outsider Designer—A Shift in Power?" and "Drake Firm Breaks Tradition." The words seem to say the world is changing, rewriting its rules. Financial blogs coldly question Seraphina's experience and Caius's unusual emotional side. Society writers enjoy the chaos, guessing what it means for the Drakes, the secret club, and the old men who still whisper behind closed doors, where power tastes like whiskey.

Caius's jaw tightens as he reads. Seraphina laughs quietly, bold and fearless.

"They act like you made me Supreme Chancellor," she says.

"Some would find that less scary," Caius replies, his eyes narrowing as he reads an article full of hidden meaning about trust and balance in the boardroom.

Seraphina looks at him sideways and smiles, then turns pages in her notebook. It's a messy plan—arrows and names circled in firm handwriting.

"Damien Pierce first," she says. "He likes to stir things up. He'll want everyone watching. He'll probably corner you in front of the Club to see if you quit."

"He'll seem friendly, then force my hand," Caius says evenly but with a hidden edge.

"Olivia Barnes," Seraphina goes on, marking her list. "She plays by the rules—process, ethics. She watches for a weakness. You respect her, but she won't let the walls fall."

"She'll start small, then drag the board in once she smells blood," Caius folds his arms, firm and ready.

Seraphina smiles tightly, flipping to the next scenario. "So do we lie low or show everything?"

"Neither," says Caius quietly. "Show only what helps us. Let them believe what they want. The Club lives on secrets; truth is what they make of it."

"Then we show the truth we want them to see," Seraphina says.

Sunlight catches her chestnut hair as she turns. A tattoo peeks from her wrist—a sign of both threat and promise. She feels the rising tension of judgment waiting just outside the boardroom, knowing that their partnership shakes the foundation of old money, traditions, and secret promises.

The Orion Club is real power in New York. Its members guard old wealth and secrets, shaping the city for generations. It's not a myth but a place of rules spoken in looks, quiet movements, and threats in a raised glass. To them, Caius and Seraphina are chaos—unruly and dangerous. Caius knows he's the traitor at his own table, the one who opened a window when all doors were locked for years. The risks are huge: not just his money, but the rules of who belongs and who controls the city's future.

Inside the Club, tensions run deep. Damien and Olivia watch closely. Damien hides doubt behind rivalry and hunger, much like Caius's own. Olivia is quieter but sharp, her alliances quick. Both belong to traditions fading as Caius breaks the rules—choosing trust over heritage, partnership over rank. The tension between the three is silent but real, shown in tiny gestures in meetings and lounges, every invite a test, every meeting a chance to prove worth.

Caius's phone buzzes on the desk. Marcus's name appears. The message is short: resistance in the Club, talks of a board revolt. Old members are worried, new ones braver since Seraphina arrived. Danger and chance—old power waking, unsure what to fight.

Seraphina moves closer, her hand on his shoulder, warm against the cool morning. She meets his steady eyes.

"They worry because we matter, because we're different. Different is what this world needs. If we stand together, their fight becomes our test."

Caius nods, her firm voice grounding him. The city's shape rises before them, raw and bright. The morning opens wide, new and scary. Their shadows blur against the dawn—armor and will combined—as the coming light pushes them forward.

The glass doors slide open quietly, and Caius steps onto the balcony, bare feet touching cold slate. His breath makes small white clouds in the chilly air. Manhattan is covered in a violet mist. Towers shine like far-off stones, their lights soft and ready. The city wakes; a distant taxi horn breaks the quiet, floating up as a sign of the day to come. He wraps a dark blanket around his shoulders and leans on the railing, muscles tense, as if the skyline commands alertness. The old scar above his brow tingles, as it always does in calm moments.

Seraphina comes out behind him, her own blanket over pajamas, hair half-tamed by the wind. She presses close, sharing warmth. Together, they watch a city both huge and very small beneath their breath. Dawn colors the clouds pink and gold, filling windows with soft light, the day's first magic.

For a long while, no one speaks. The air smells faintly of ozone and baked bread from a midnight bakery. Early joggers become dark shapes on the painted sky. Caius listens to the city's beat and to himself—old plans clashing with a new desire for something unplanned and real. He thinks about legacy, what a new empire could mean—not just stone and contracts, but ideas and change.

"There was a time," he says softly, "when I thought the only way to leave a mark was to conquer. Buy, build, take over—make the world match my dreams. But standing here..." He touches her arm, steady and sure. "I want to build a foundation that doesn't ask for surrender. I want a legacy strong enough to challenge what came before. Not just for my name, but for something lasting and kind."

Seraphina thinks about his words and the colors breaking the horizon. She grips the blanket tighter, her eyes bright and strong. "A legacy that means more than power or money. That's why I'm here." Her laugh is soft and real. "I want to create with you, not just follow. Make work that's honest and wild—bring art to parts of this city no one expects. I need to keep who I am while we build something new."

The city seems to listen, pausing on their words. The future hangs between them, bright and unsure. The streets below glow with slow-moving headlights. Caius sets his jaw, imagining boardrooms changed—tables filled not just with suits but with voices long ignored. He pictures galleries in the company halls, strength measured by more than money.

Seraphina nudges him, smiling a little crooked but true. "We'll have to face them—all of them. The Orion Club won't want change. The press will twist our words; every mistake will be used against us. Sometimes I wonder if love is enough to stop us from becoming what they expect."

He looks at a mist-covered skyscraper, memories of fights and whispers coming back. Doubts flicker—failures, betrayals, warnings that being open is a weakness. But her certainty, the stubborn light in her eyes, sparks something alive beneath his fear.

"The thorns won't disappear," he says quietly. "There are wounds from the past—mine and yours. Scars the world would reopen given a chance. But flames need fuel." He threads his fingers through hers, steady and bright. "I'll take the fire over silence. If we burn together, maybe something new can live."

Seraphina's thumb makes a soft circle on his hand. They say nothing. As the mist lifts, the sun lights their joined hands, outlining them in gold. The city breathes—a subway rumbles, a market opens, a vendor calls. Caius hears hope in these sounds: maybe, together, they can change power's shape, direct the energy of a city built on secrets and deals.

What will their days be like if they succeed? He sees a future shaped by their ideas—color and glass, new rules welcoming change, partnerships that bring poetry as well as money. Maybe there is hope in trying, in not backing down from resistance. Maybe there is meaning in every morning they choose to face it together.

They turn side by side to watch the sun rise—a bright line against the city's sharp edges. In the quiet, surrounded by gold and lights, they say nothing. Their promise is silent but strong, carried on the wind above the waking world. Hope, fear, and excitement fill the air as day begins—a promise as fragile and fierce as dawn itself.

Epilogue

The city burned with light, a restless hum that never slept. Caius stood at the floor-to-ceiling window of his penthouse, Seraphina's head resting against his chest, her warmth steadying the storm inside him. For the first time in years, he allowed himself to believe in something fragile. Something worth keeping.

But men like him never held on to peace for long.

The phone on the table vibrated once, a sharp reminder that the world outside these walls still demanded him. A name glowed across the screen.

Lucien Blackwell.

Caius's jaw tightened. Manhattan's most feared defense attorney wasn't one to call without cause. If Lucien needed him, it meant shadows were already gathering—and tomorrow's courthouse battle would draw them all deeper into the fire.

Caius pressed a kiss to Seraphina's hair, a vow unspoken. He might have found love, but the Brotherhood's storms were only beginning.

Final Thoughts

Thank you for walking through the shadows of the Orion Brotherhood, where power, loyalty, and love collide in ways that can change everything. Each brother carries his own secrets, his own scars, and his own story waiting to be told.

This book was just the beginning. Behind every closed door of the Brotherhood lies another vow to be tested, another love too dangerous to resist, and another man who will discover that even the strongest fall when their hearts are on the line.

If this story moved you, I'd be deeply grateful if you shared your thoughts by leaving a review. Every word you share helps other readers find their way into the Brotherhood—and keeps these stories alive.

Until the next brother steps into the light...
—C.K. Franco

Review Request

LOVED the Orion Dynasty Book Series?

<u>Click here to leave your review on Amazon.</u>

Your review helps this dark billionaire romance world reach new readers who crave power, passion, and redemption.

Or type this link into your browser:

https://www.amazon.com/review/create-review?asin=B0FPBNNPZN